MOON OVER BUFFALO

MOON
OVER
BUFFALO

A *Comedy* by
KEN LUDWIG

GARDEN CITY, NEW YORK

Design by Maria Chiarino
Manufactured in the U.S.A.
ISBN: 1-56865-201-1

MOON OVER BUFFALO premiered on Broadway at the Martin Beck Theatre on October 1, 1995. It was produced by Elizabeth Williams, Heidi Landesman, DLT Entertainment Ltd., Hal Luftig and Jujamcyn Theatres. It was directed by Tom Moore. The set was designed by Heidi Landesman, the costumes by Bob Mackie, the lighting by Ken Billington and the sound by Tony Meola. The fights were staged by B.H. Barry. General Management was by 101 Productions, Ltd., the Production Supervisor was Steven Beckler, and the Stage Manager was Tom Capps. The cast was as follows:

Ethel . . . . Jane Connell

Rosalind . . . . Randy Graff

Howard . . . . Andy Taylor

George Hay . . . . Philip Bosco

Charlotte Hay . . . . Carol Burnett

Eileen . . . . Kate Miller

Paul . . . . Dennis Ryan

Richard Maynard . . . . James Valentine

Understudies: Richard Poe, Jane Sell Trese, Lannyl Stephens and David Beach.

Place and time:
On stage and backstage at the Erlanger
Theatre, Buffalo, N.Y., 1953

ACT ONE
A mid-morning in June

ACT TWO
Scene One: Two hours later
Scene Two: Immediately following
Scene Three: Two hours later

In loving memory of my father, Jacob S. Ludwig, 1913–1990, who would have loved this play.

ACT ONE

A fusillade of musket and cannon, the bloody cries of a pitched battle—and as the lights come up, we're at the Siege of Arras in 1640, at the outpost of the Company of Carbon de Castel-Jaloux. But we're not, really. We're on the stage of the Erlanger Theatre in Buffalo, New York, during a rehearsal of Act IV of Cyrano de Bergerac. *The stage is full of smoke, noise and tattered flags, and the actors are in silhouette. George and Charlotte Hay are playing Cyrano and Roxane, and the rest of the parts are played by members of their company.*

CONFUSED VOICES: "Retreat! For God's sake retreat!"

FIRST SOLDIER: "Sound the alarm!"

SECOND SOLDIER: "We are all dead!"

DE GUICHE: "Retreat!"

THIRD SOLDIER: "Retreat!"

THREE SOLDIERS: "Retreat!"

CYRANO (GEORGE): "No! Never! Not in this life!"

DE GUICHE: "You fool, we shall all die! It is ten to one against us!"

CYRANO (GEORGE): "Be damned your numbers! And damn you! I am Cyrano de Bergerac!"

THREE SOLDIERS (*weakly*): "Yay."

GEORGE: Stop! Stop!!

(*The music stops and we go to work lights*)

GEORGE: For the hundredth time, I want the cheer louder! The audience won't hear you! Let's try it again. "I am Cyrano de Bergerac!"

THREE SOLDIERS (*weakly*): "Yay!"

GEORGE (*disgusted, turning away*): I don't know why we even bother rehearsing. . . . Louder!

THREE SOLDIERS: *"Yay!"*

GEORGE: That's better. All right, let's run it.

(*The music and lights restore to performance level*)

DE GUICHE: "You fool, we shall all die! It is ten to one against us!"

CYRANO (GEORGE): "Be damned your numbers! And damn you! I am Cyrano de Bergerac!"

THREE SOLDIERS (*weakly*): "Yay."

DE GUICHE: "Popinjay!"

(*De Guiche walks off in a huff. We hear the sound of a horse and carriage approaching*)

SECOND SOLDIER: "Halt, who goes there?!"

FIRST SOLDIER: "It's a coach!"

THIRD SOLDIER: "What?!"

FIRST SOLDIER: "In the camp?!"

(*Off, the horse whinnies*)

SECOND SOLDIER: "Look! 'Tis Roxane!"

(*Roxane enters with a basket of fruit, and the Soldiers cheer*)

THREE SOLDIERS (*weakly*): "Yay!"

(*George gives them a look*)

SECOND SOLDIER: "She brings supplies!"

FIRST SOLDIER: "Bread!"

SECOND SOLDIER: "And wine!"

THIRD SOLDIER: "And chicken!"

(*Roxane exits*)

LE BRET (PAUL): "Cyrano! That was the Comte de Guiche you insulted! Stop trying to be the Three Musketeers in one!"

(*During the following oration, Ethel, an actress in her 70s, enters from the wings. She's dressed in her everyday 1950s clothes, and therefore looks incongruous*)

CYRANO (GEORGE): "What would you have me do? Hanh?!"

Seek for the patronage of some great man,
And like a creeping vine on a tall tree
Crawl upward, where I cannot stand alone?
No thank you!"

ETHEL: Oh my God, I've seen more talent at a dog show.

(Ethel joins in the speech with George. After a line or two, we hear only Ethel, and the "onstage" action fades away. Simultaneously, she makes her way to the green room of the Erlanger Theatre.*

The room is large, comfortable, and a bit shabby. It contains a chaise, a large pouffe, and one or two easy chairs. It's decorated with Theatre posters and other theatrical bric-a-brac. Stage right is a door to the street; stage left, two doors to the backstage area, one of them up a short flight of steps. Up center is another door to the backstage area and also a door to a utility closet. The time is a mid-morning in June, 1953.

When Ethel enters the room, she continues playing Cyrano, even as she potters around straightening things up)

GEORGE/ETHEL:
    "Dedicate, as others do,
    Poems to pawnbrokers? Be a buffoon
    In the vile hope of teasing out a smile
    On some cold face?"

* See Appendix A

ETHEL:

"Eat a toad

For breakfast every morning?

Wear out my belly grovelling in the dust?

No thank you!

But,"

(*Rosalind enters from the street door, carrying a suit-case. She's bright and attractive, in her early 30s. She sees Ethel and smiles with affection. Ethel is facing the other way and can't see Rosalind. Also, as we'll soon realize, Ethel is quite deaf and is never aware of very much unless it's in front of her and shouting*)

ETHEL:

"To sing, to laugh, to dream,

To walk in my own way and be alone,

Free, with an eye to see things as they are."

ROZ: Grandma.

ETHEL: "To travel any road under the sun,"

ROZ: *Grandma!*

ETHEL: "Nor doubt if fame or fortune . . ."

ROZ: *Grandma!!*

ETHEL (*startled, then overjoyed*): Oh! . . . Rosalind! Dearest girl! What a surprise! You're getting more beautiful every day. (*A big hug*) You look adorable!

ROZ: So do you.

ETHEL: What?

ROZ (*louder*): So do you! You look great!

ETHEL: I'm afraid you'll have to speak up, dear.

ROZ: *Grandma, can I get you your hearing aid?!*

ETHEL (*fondly*): No thank you, dear, I'm not in the mood for lemonade. Oh, I miss you terribly. It isn't the same here without you.

ROZ: *I miss you too, Grandma. Hey! How is the tour going? Do you like Buffalo?*

ETHEL: No. I don't. It stinks. If it wasn't named for an animal, it would have nothing going for it.

ROZ: Grandma . . .

ETHEL: I don't mind so much for myself, really, but it's quite a come-down for your mother. She played Broadway, you know, in the forties. Then your father dragged her down to his level.

ROZ: Grandma!

ETHEL: Revivals of tired old plays. B-movies. You should have heard him doing Cyrano just now at the dress rehearsal. The man is a walking ham. They should stick cloves in him and serve him with pineapple.

ROZ: *Grandma, listen! I have a surprise. I'm getting married.*

(*It takes a moment to sink in . . . then Roz and Ethel squeal with delight, like schoolgirls, and hug each other*)

ETHEL: Oh, Rosalind, how wonderful! I've always said that you and Paul were made for each other.

ROZ: It isn't Paul.

ETHEL: The boy has spunk . . .

ROZ: *Grandma, it's not Paul! Paul and I broke up!*

ETHEL: . . . It isn't Paul?

ROZ: *No!*

ETHEL: Well that's a mistake. (*Roz sighs; here it comes*) You look ravishing on the stage together. You could do all the great couples . . .

ROZ: *Grandma, I'm not an actress anymore! I'm in advertising!*

ETHEL: Yes, I know, and it's revolting.

ROZ: *Don't you remember the talk we had at Christmas?!*

ETHEL: . . . No.

ROZ (*really pouring her heart out*): Grandma, this is *your* life. And Mother and Dad's. And that's fine. I'm very proud of you. But I grew up with it. I want something different. Something that doesn't drive me crazy all the time. Does that make any sense?

ETHEL (*fondly*): Rosalind, dearest, can I tell you something?

ROZ: Sure.

ETHEL: I haven't heard a single word you've said.

ROZ: . . . *Grandma, can I please get you your hearing
aid!!!*

ETHEL: All right. Fine. *One glass.* . . . Now listen to
me, young lady. The theatre may be dying. The
glamorous invalid may be crawling through the des-
ert with but a single lung in its feeble chest, but it is
still breathing and it is all we've got. It is our lifeline
to humanity. Without it, we would all be Republi-
cans. I'm very tired now, dear, and I'm going to lie
down. (*At the door*) It's wonderful having you back.

(*She exits. Roz runs to the door and shouts*)

ROZ: *Grandma! I love you!*

(*At which moment, we hear a knock at the street door*)

ROZ: Come in. (. . . *knock knock knock*) Come in!
(. . . *knock knock knock; angry*) *Would you come in,
please, the door's open!!*

(*Howard enters. He's in his late 20s, very good-natured
and quite good-looking. At the moment, he's rather
frightened*)

HOWARD: . . . Sweetheart?

ROZ: Hi, honey. Come on in.

(*They kiss*)

HOWARD: Are your parents here?

ROZ: I don't think so.

HOWARD (*relieved*): Oh, good.

ROZ: Howard . . .

HOWARD: Well I'm sorry. You know how I feel about this. "Meeting the in-laws." It makes me nervous.

ROZ: You have nothing to worry about.

HOWARD: I'd be all right if they weren't such . . . big stars. The glamorous life . . .

ROZ: Howard, does this look glamorous? (*Indicating the room*)

HOWARD (*looking around*): . . . Well, yeah. It does.

ROZ: This is Buffalo, New York. It's like . . . Scranton without the charm.

HOWARD: I was born here, actually.

ROZ: Oh.

HOWARD: I like Scranton, too.

ROZ: Howard, the point is, it's not Broadway. And they're doing rep!

HOWARD: Right. . . . What's "rep" again?

ROZ: More than one play. In repertory. They alternate. Right now it's *Private Lives* by Noel Coward and *Cyrano de Bergerac*. Only they've cut down *Cyrano* for a small company. They do it with five actors.

HOWARD: Aha. The sort of . . . one-nostril version.

(*He laughs; then sighs with anxiety*)

ROZ: It's sort of sweet that you're nervous about meeting them.

HOWARD: Nervous? Look at me, I'm a wreck! Do they know that I'm in show business, too?

ROZ: Howard, you're not exactly in show business. I mean, they wouldn't think of it as show business.

HOWARD: Oh. (*Beat*) I am on television.

ROZ: You're a weatherman.

HOWARD: Right. I mean, it's kind of acting, like your parents.

ROZ: Howard, they do Shakespeare. And Chekhov. You do precipitation.

HOWARD (*glum*): Yeah, I know . . .

ROZ: Howard, I'm very proud of you. It's a wonderful job. We can settle down and have children . . .

HOWARD: I love children. I want to have six, at least.

ROZ: Let's start with one.

HOWARD: Okay.

ROZ: Now listen to me. I want you to be very, very nice to them. Tell them how much you admire their work.

HOWARD: Well I *do!* I mean, my God, when I was a kid, they were on the cover of *Life* magazine. "Shakespeare on Broadway . . ."

ROZ: "Look Out Barrymores, Here Come the Hays." They had it reproduced on their china.

HOWARD: Wow.

ROZ: Then they had two big flops in a row and went to Hollywood.

HOWARD: Yeah, I know. I saw every movie they ever made!

ROZ: Good . . .

HOWARD: "Sergeant Yukon," "Apache Woman . . ." (*Suddenly*) Oh my God! I forgot the bag!

ROZ: What bag?

HOWARD: I have a surprise for your father. When I was in New York last week, I read in the paper about an auction. They were selling off props and stuff from one of the big studios and . . . well, I bought one of your father's old costumes. I thought he'd like it.

ROZ: That is so sweet! Which one did you get?

HOWARD: General George S. Patton! Wait'll you see it! The trouble is, I don't have anything for your mother yet. I guess she wouldn't take cash . . . ?

ROZ: Howard. They will love you for who you are.

HOWARD: What if I freeze up?! I-I-I do that sometimes, when I'm nervous! I can't even remember my own . . . *name.*

ROZ: You'll be fine! I promise! (*A kiss*) All right?

HOWARD: . . . All right.

ROZ: I'll see if they're in their dressing rooms.

HOWARD: I'll go with you.

ROZ: You stay here, in case they show up.

HOWARD: I'd rather go with you . . .

ROZ: Howard, stay! Nothing's going to happen in two minutes!

(*She exits. Pause. He looks around the room. He spies a Cyrano hat on the table. He picks it up and puts it on.*

He preens. When he takes off the hat, a Cyrano nose drops out to the floor. He picks it up and looks at it with curiosity—then suspicion. He moves it down towards his crotch . . . is that what it is?! At this moment, George Hay bursts through the center door, still wearing his Cyrano costume, nose, and makeup, brandishing a sword)*

GEORGE: CHYAA!

(Just as suddenly, Charlotte Hay bursts through the door at the top of the stairs. She's still dressed as Roxane, and she also has a sword)

CHARLOTTE: CHYAA!

(George and Charlotte face off—then start fencing in the best Errol Flynn tradition. This is their daily exercise, as well as their fun)

GEORGE: Aroint thee, villain!

CHARLOTTE: Stay back, thou knave and cutpurse!

GEORGE: Stand thy ground, I say, or thou shalt bleed from ear to ear like the vomiting stream at flood tide!

(More sword play. Howard watches with his mouth hanging open)

CHARLOTTE: Dungheap!

GEORGE: Witch!

* See Appendix B

CHARLOTTE: Bull's pizzle!

(*The next exchange brings the combatants nose to nose, their swords crossed—then suddenly Charlotte stamps on George's foot to get the advantage*)

GEORGE: Ow!

CHARLOTTE: Ha!

GEORGE: Villain!

(*They're at it again. Then they both notice Howard for the first time and stop fighting*)

CHARLOTTE: What is this?

GEORGE: I know not, but 'tis passing strange.

HOWARD (*waves*): . . . Hi.

(*Charlotte lunges at George, George counters, then grabs Howard around the neck in a hammerlock, with his sword at Howard's throat*)

CHARLOTTE: Ha!

GEORGE: Ha!

HOWARD: Argh!

GEORGE: Stay back, I say, or the lad shall die!

CHARLOTTE: Coward!

GEORGE: If thou dost move *one inch*, the lad shall spout blood like a fountain.

(*Howard is terrified. He tries to chuckle, to be a good sport*)

HOWARD (*to Charlotte*): . . . Don't move.

(*Charlotte lunges—*)

CHARLOTTE: Ha!

GEORGE: Ha!

(*—and George discards Howard like a sack of potatoes. Howard careens off a chair. Then George and Charlotte go at it again, and exit fighting*)

CHARLOTTE: Hold up thy head, vile Scot!

GEORGE: I'll make a ghost of him that lets me!

(*And they're gone. Howard gets to his feet, panting. After a beat, Roz enters at the top of the stairs*)

ROZ: They're not in their dressing rooms.

HOWARD: I-I-I-I-

ROZ: Howard?

HOWARD: I have to go now.

(*He heads for the street door*)

ROZ: Where are you going?

HOWARD: I need a few minutes. I'll be back.

ROZ: Howard, what's wrong?

HOWARD: I have to think about this! You don't just-just-just rush into a relationship! It takes some thinking!!

(*He exits*)

ROZ: Howard! Are you crazy?! (*Exiting*) Get back here!!

(*She runs out. A moment later, George and Charlotte reenter in high spirits*)

GEORGE: Do you know what I like most about the author of *Cyrano?* He's dead, so he can't argue with me. (*Charlotte laughs*) Now listen, I have a new idea for tomorrow. When the carriage arrives, during the battle, and you step out, I want you to pause, curtsey to the soldiers—and I'm going to put a spotlight on your face to suggest that you have descended like an angel from the heavens.

CHARLOTTE: Oh, George, let's try it! Now!

GEORGE: All right.

CHARLOTTE: Clip-clop clip-clop clip-clop. Na-a-a-y. (*A whinny*)

GEORGE: "Halt, who goes there?!"

CHARLOTTE: "It's a coach!"

GEORGE: "What? In the camp?!"

CHARLOTTE: "Look! 'Tis Roxane!"

GEORGE: "Thank God!"

CHARLOTTE (*weakly*): "Yay." (*She steps elegantly down the last two steps of the stairway*) And I float down, out of the carriage, like an angel from heaven . . .

GEORGE: Spotlight!

CHARLOTTE (*as Roxane*): "Good morning, gentlemen."

GEORGE: "Roxane, on the King's service?!"

CHARLOTTE: "Yes. In the service of my own king: Love."

GEORGE: That's it! It'll make the scene!

CHARLOTTE: "Cyrano. My best friend. I need your help."

GEORGE (*as Cyrano, kneeling, taking her hand*): "I am at your disposal, madam, now and forever."

(*He kisses her hand and lays his cheek upon it*)

CHARLOTTE (*moved*): When you do that, George, center stage, in front of a thousand people holding their breath, I wet myself. I can't help it.

GEORGE: Thank you, my darling.

CHARLOTTE: Kiss me. Now. Before the moment passes.

(*She lifts his nose and kisses him on the lips. They start necking on the chaise—when Ethel enters from backstage*)

ETHEL: Don't mind me, I'm just the hired help.

GEORGE: Well, well, if it isn't the Hound of the Baskervilles.

(*During the following, George and Charlotte remove their* Cyrano *clothes and put on their relaxing clothes. Charlotte, of course, looks stunning. Ethel gathers up their costumes to take them away*)

CHARLOTTE (*to George*): Don't start.

GEORGE: Oh, she can't hear a thing I'm saying. She hasn't heard a word in twenty years. (*To Ethel*) Have you, Quasimodo?

CHARLOTTE: George, stop it.

GEORGE: Tell me, Ethel, have you frightened any little children lately? Offered them a ride on your broomstick?

CHARLOTTE: George . . .

GEORGE: I cannot believe, to this day, that *that* is your mother. Here you are, the greatest stage actress in a generation, and you were spawned by a troll?

CHARLOTTE: George, cut it out.

GEORGE: You must have been switched at birth. Somewhere out there is Ethel's real daughter, traveling with Ringling Brothers, as the Wolf Woman of Borneo.

CHARLOTTE (*as Ethel starts to exit heaped with the bundle of clothes*): Thank you, Mother!

GEORGE: *Thank you, Mother!*

ETHEL (*as she goes out the door*): George, my hearing aid is in, now grow up!

(*She exits, and George slams the door, hurting his back*)

GEORGE: *Ow!* God, my back! Am I getting old, Charlotte?

CHARLOTTE: No, dear, you're just falling apart.

GEORGE (*bitterly*): No wonder they didn't want me for the *Pimpernel* movie.

CHARLOTTE: Us, dear, they didn't want us.

GEORGE: We were *this close*, Charlotte. I could taste it! George and Charlotte Hay in the new Frank Capra production, *The Twilight of the Scarlet Pimpernel*. It would have put us right back on top.

CHARLOTTE: There will be other movies.

GEORGE: Not like this one! We were perfect for it! (*Beat*) No wonder Hollywood is such a cesspool. I mean, please. *Frank Capra* directs *The Twilight of The Scarlet Pimpernel*???

CHARLOTTE: I know. I agree with you.

GEORGE: Comedies. Fine. Christmas movies. But *The Scarlet Pimpernel*?!

CHARLOTTE: I didn't even get to meet him.

GEORGE: Nor did I. Nor do I care to, may he rot in hell.

CHARLOTTE: I can see it now. "Mr. Pimpernel Goes To Washington."

GEORGE: Exactly! Ow!

CHARLOTTE: Get down, George. I'll work on your back.

(*During the following, George sits next to the chaise and Charlotte massages his neck and shoulders*)

GEORGE: You do realize they started filming yesterday. At this very moment, the cameras are rolling and Ronald Colman is wearing *my tights*.

CHARLOTTE (*calmly, as the massage continues*): Oh George, let them have their Ronald Colman and their Greer Garson. Who gives a damn.

GEORGE: You're right.

CHARLOTTE: I'm sure that Miss Garson will do a perfectly adequate job.

GEORGE: You're right.

CHARLOTTE: If that's what they want.

GEORGE: I agree entirely.

CHARLOTTE: . . . Stupid little bitch. (*George laughs*) I met her once. Did you know that? (*With increasing bitterness*) She was filming *Pride and Prejudice* and I was next door filming *Apache Woman.* She was cutting the crusts off little tea sandwiches, and I was boiling a pig in a teepee.

GEORGE: Charlotte—

CHARLOTTE: She was making love to Laurence Olivier, and I was sacrificing a chicken with Chief Chunkachook. (*She starts chanting an Indian war chant, beating on his back with the edges of her hands*) Hiya hiya hiya hiya . . .

GEORGE (*overlapping*): Charlotte . . . Charlotte!

(*She stops*)

CHARLOTTE: How's your back?

GEORGE: Better. But don't stop.

(*The massage continues. George is relaxing. He's almost asleep*)

CHARLOTTE: George?

GEORGE: Hm?

CHARLOTTE: Can I ask you a question?

GEORGE: Mm.

CHARLOTTE: Did you sleep with Eileen?

(*He sits up with a start*)

GEORGE: Charlotte! How can you say such a thing?!

CHARLOTTE: I've seen how you look at her.

GEORGE: She's a pretty girl. I'm not dead.

CHARLOTTE: Not yet. I know exactly when it happened, George. We were in the middle of that terrible fight.

GEORGE: And whose fault was that?

CHARLOTTE: It was your fault, dear. You called me the world's oldest living ingenue.

GEORGE: I merely mentioned that a woman in her fifties should not try to play Saint Joan. It's like watching Eleanor Roosevelt play Peter Pan.

CHARLOTTE: I happen to admire Eleanor Roosevelt.

GEORGE: So do I, but I don't want to watch her fly out the window.

CHARLOTTE: You're changing the subject.

GEORGE: For heaven's sake, Eileen barely knows I exist.

CHARLOTTE: Oh, please. When you walk into the room she starts to glow. I could use her for a reading lamp.

GEORGE: You are off your rocker. It's extraordinary. It is unkind.

CHARLOTTE: George, I don't mind as long as you tell me the truth! Did you sleep with her or didn't you?! Yes or no?!

GEORGE: . . . *No!!!* All right?! The answer is no!!

CHARLOTTE (*skeptically*): Really?

GEORGE: Oh, it's killing you about the film, isn't it.

CHARLOTTE: Don't be silly. That has nothing to do with it.

GEORGE: Scarlet Pimpernel, Scarlet Pimpernel.

CHARLOTTE: Oh, stop it.

GEORGE: *Greer Garson!*

CHARLOTTE: Don't be an idiot!*

GEORGE: I'm sure it's slaying you to be stuck out here in Siberia while Miss Garson swans around the set in Hollywood like the Queen of Sheba.

CHARLOTTE: George—

* See Author's Note.

GEORGE: I'm sure you had fantastical visions of being slobbered over by a legion of toadies, having your ears powdered.

CHARLOTTE: All right, George, I'm sorry!

GEORGE (*the injured husband*): *Well it's too late now, isn't it?! You have hurt my feelings!*

CHARLOTTE: . . . Oh stop it, I did not.

GEORGE: You did so.

CHARLOTTE: Did not.

GEORGE: *You did so!*

(*Pause*)

CHARLOTTE: Well I know how to fix it.

GEORGE (*knowing what's coming*): Charlotte, don't.

CHARLOTTE: It always works.

GEORGE: Not this time!

(*She sits on his lap and starts to tickle him*)

CHARLOTTE: Tickle, tickle, tickle!

GEORGE (*laughing*): Stop it!

CHARLOTTE: Tickle, tickle, tickle!

GEORGE (*laughing*): Charlotte! I'm warning you—!

CHARLOTTE: Tickle, tickle, tickle, tickle, tickle, tickle, tickle—!

(*They're having a wonderful, intimate time tickling and laughing . . . when Eileen walks in from the street. She's young and very beautiful. They see her and stop cold*)

GEORGE: Eileen!

CHARLOTTE: Good morning.

(*Beat. Eileen bursts into tears and runs across the room and out the door to the dressing rooms*)

GEORGE: Eileen! Wait! Eileen!

(*George stands up and hurries to the door—and Charlotte rolls off his lap to the floor. Then she stands up and looks at him with blood in her eye*)

GEORGE: Don't look at me like that.

CHARLOTTE: Fine. I'll go talk to her.

GEORGE: I'll do it! You have caused enough trouble for one morning. (*Exiting*) Eileen!

(*The moment he's gone, Paul enters from the street. He's in his 30s, good-looking in a rough-and-ready sort of way, and very likeable*)

CHARLOTTE: Hello, Paul.

PAUL: What's with Eileen? She walked right past me. I think she was crying.

CHARLOTTE: Well, she was born in Buffalo. Maybe she suddenly realized she's still here.

PAUL: Actually, she loves it here. She started out here in the theatre, but what she really wants to do is television.

CHARLOTTE: Oh, please.

PAUL: She could do all right on TV. She's pretty. Wholesome.

CHARLOTTE: Wholesome isn't the word. She could give milk.

PAUL: . . . Charlotte. Have you talked to Roz lately?

CHARLOTTE: Last Sunday. I brought up your name and she started screaming.

PAUL: Oh, great.

CHARLOTTE: I never understood why you two broke up.

PAUL: Oh, she wanted me to give up the theatre so she could lead a "normal life." (*He shakes his head and laughs*) Can you imagine anyone in your family being normal?!

(*Charlotte starts to laugh . . . then stops and gives him a look. At which moment, Roz enters from the street*)

ROZ: Hi, Mother.

CHARLOTTE: Pumpkin! Sweetie! (*They hug*) When did you get here?!

ROZ: A few minutes ago.

CHARLOTTE: We were just talking about you. This second!

(*The following exchange is rapid and monotone, anger overlaid with social intercourse*)

ROZ: Hello Paul.

PAUL: Hi Roz.

ROZ: How's show biz?

PAUL: Great I've never been happier.

ROZ: Well good for you I'm thrilled.

PAUL: Thanks.

ROZ: You're welcome.

(*Pause*)

CHARLOTTE: . . . This is going well.

ROZ: I thought you were in New York.

PAUL: I came back to work for your parents.

ROZ: How nice.

PAUL: I'll check on Eileen.

(*Paul exits*)

CHARLOTTE: Rosalind, why don't you two just get married and get it over with.

ROZ: I wish you would stop trying to run my life. It's my life, not your life!

CHARLOTTE: You're right. I'm sorry. You're right. (*Pause. The wounded mother*) I'm only the one who gave birth to you.

ROZ: Mother . . .

CHARLOTTE: Twelve pounds, fourteen ounces. . . . They needed a forklift.

ROZ: Mother!

(*George enters*)

GEORGE: She locked herself in, she . . . Rosalind! My baby!

ROZ: Daddy!

(*She runs to him and they hug*)

GEORGE: How's my little girl? . . . Charlotte, how is it possible that two such plain people as ourselves could produce an offspring as beautiful as this one?

CHARLOTTE: . . . She's not yours. I slept around.

GEORGE: Roz, have you come to your senses? You could step right back into the company.

ROZ: No thank you. That's not why I'm here. I have a surprise for everybody, but I lost it.

GEORGE (*calling through the door*): Paul, get in here! Look who's arrived!

ROZ: Daddy! God. Don't you two ever stop? . . . Look, I'll see you later, I've got to go.

GEORGE: Roz . . . .

(*Roz exits and Paul enters*)

PAUL: . . . She's gone?

GEORGE: She heard your name and fled into the Forest of Arden. You do have a way with women, Paul.

PAUL: Thanks.

CHARLOTTE: And how is Little Miss Eileen?

PAUL: She wouldn't open the door for me either. I wonder what happened.

CHARLOTTE: She's in love with George.

GEORGE: Charlotte, would you please keep your menopausal hallucinations to yourself. The girl is obviously in some distress.

PAUL: I'll go try again.

GEORGE: Yes, do. You are the Company Manager.

PAUL: I'm also your second lead this week.

GEORGE: I beg your pardon?

PAUL: Webster quit this morning. He packed his bags and left.

GEORGE: He can't do that! I'll sue the untalented little weasel!

CHARLOTTE: Why on earth would he just leave?

PAUL: Because he wasn't paid for two weeks.

GEORGE: Well none of us has been paid for two weeks! What kind of feeble excuse is that?!

CHARLOTTE: Nobody told me about this.

GEORGE: Well Paul just told you, didn't he, the big blabbermouth.

PAUL: Sorry. By the way, have you talked to your agent this morning? He called twice.

GEORGE: I have an agent? Surely you jest. Didn't you read about it in *Scientific American?* The day my checks went down to four digits, he vanished from the face of the earth.

(*Paul exits*)

CHARLOTTE (*gently*): George . . . talk to me. Are we in trouble?

GEORGE: Oh, we'll make it. We'll survive. We always do. It's television that's killing us. Entertainment by the yard. It's putting us out of business.

CHARLOTTE: George . . .

GEORGE: What's the matter with these people? Don't they care anymore?! Don't they know the difference?!

(*There's a knock on the street door*)

GEORGE: I'm not here. You haven't seen me.

CHARLOTTE: George!

GEORGE: If it's a native Buffalonian, offer it water and some long grass, maybe it'll go away.

(*He exits. Knock knock knock*)

CHARLOTTE: I'm coming!

(*She opens the door and Howard is there*)

CHARLOTTE: Yes?

HOWARD: Hi.

CHARLOTTE (*annoyed*): What do you want?

HOWARD: I-I-I just want to tell you before you say anything else, that I think you're the most wonderful
actress that ever lived!

CHARLOTTE (*suddenly the soul of gracious-
ness*): . . . Please, come in. I'm Charlotte Hay.

HOWARD (*extending his hand*): Hi. I'm . . . I'm uh
. . . I'm uh . . . (*He turns white; his worst night-
mare is happening; he's forgotten his name*) Oh my
God!

(*He buries his face in his hands—as Richard Maynard
enters through the open street door. He is a loveable,
good-looking man in his fifties, in a conservative suit
and tie*)

RICHARD: Knock knock.

CHARLOTTE: Richard!

(*She runs to him and embraces him*)

RICHARD: Hello, Charlotte.

CHARLOTTE: What a wonderful surprise!

RICHARD (*to Howard, who has looked up*): How do you
do. Richard Maynard. You are . . . ?

CHARLOTTE: I wouldn't ask him that. Apparently it's a
trick question.

HOWARD: Are you famous, too?!

RICHARD: No, but apparently I remind some people of Loretta Young.

CHARLOTTE: Mr. Maynard is our lawyer and represents every major star in Hollywood.

HOWARD: Wow.

RICHARD: Who's your favorite? Besides Charlotte, of course?

HOWARD: Esther Williams. Do you know her?!

RICHARD (*nods*): I taught her to swim.

HOWARD: Wow!

CHARLOTTE: I'm awfully sorry, but do you think you could possibly come back another time?

HOWARD: Oh. Sure . . .

CHARLOTTE (*helping him out the door*): It was stunning meeting you. Whoever you are.

HOWARD (*as the door closes in his face*): Wait! I remember! It's How . . . (*The door is closed*)

CHARLOTTE: Richard, what are you doing here?!

RICHARD: Well, I was sitting in my office this morning, making a great deal of money, and I suddenly realized that I was terribly bored. So I thought, what can I do to cheer myself up. Well, I considered raising my billing rate, that usually works, but then I thought no, I would much rather take Charlotte to lunch.

CHARLOTTE: So you flew here all the way from New York City?

RICHARD (*nods*): I was in a plane, of course.

CHARLOTTE (*hugging him*): Oh, Richard, you're such a darling. I accept. In fact, I could use some cheering up myself.

RICHARD: What has the brute done this time?

CHARLOTTE: I'm not sure. Maybe it's nothing. Maybe I'm just tired.

RICHARD: Well of course you're tired! It's inhuman the way he drags you around from one city to another.

CHARLOTTE: On top of everything else, I just found out that we're not meeting our payroll.

RICHARD: Oh, I know that.

CHARLOTTE: You do?

RICHARD: It's quite serious. I've told George for months to start cutting down expenses.

CHARLOTTE: Is there anything *I* can do?

RICHARD: Well, you could do a movie. Or better yet, some television.

CHARLOTTE: We could try a different play. *Pygmalion* always makes money . . .

RICHARD: Charlotte. Halloo in there. It's 1953. The road is dead. The only stars left touring anymore, besides you two, are Cornell and the Lunts, and they have a combined age of one thousand four hundred and sixty-two.

CHARLOTTE: Well what am I supposed to do?!

RICHARD: Well, for starters, you can marry me. I've got tons of money and no one to spend it on. Except a cat with a thyroid problem. He's getting very large. I had some friends in last night, they thought I'd bought a new sofa.

CHARLOTTE: Would you be serious.

RICHARD: I'm being serious. I'll have to move out soon.

CHARLOTTE: Richard!

RICHARD (*suddenly very serious*): Charlotte, listen at me. (*Pause*) I'm not very good at this. I cannot lie the way most men do and tell you that your cheeks remind me of damask. I don't know what the hell damask is. But you really do deserve better than this. Let me pamper you a little. We can take a cruise together. Anywhere you want in the entire world. Rochester. Schenectady . . .

(*Charlotte laughs*)

CHARLOTTE: Oh, Richard, you make me very happy.

RICHARD: Good. You deserve it. And frankly, so do I. I'm tired of living alone.

CHARLOTTE: What about George?

RICHARD: No, I don't want to live with him.

CHARLOTTE (*laughing*): Richard . . .

RICHARD: Oh, I do love you so much. You're all I think about anymore.

CHARLOTTE: Richard . . .

RICHARD: Charlotte . . .

(*He's about to kiss her, when we hear Paul's urgent voice*)

PAUL (*off*): *George!!*

(*Richard and Charlotte move guiltily apart, as Paul hurries in*)

PAUL: Oh, hi. Hi.

RICHARD: How do you do. Richard Maynard, lawyer to the stars.

PAUL: Paul Singer, schlepper for two stars. Where's George?

CHARLOTTE: In his dressing room, I think.

PAUL (*worried*): He's not there.

CHARLOTTE: Is something the matter?

PAUL: No! No . . .

CHARLOTTE: Paul . . .

PAUL: There's nothing the matter! I . . . I have a question.

(*She stares right through him, but decides to leave it*)

CHARLOTTE: When you find him, tell him I'll be out for the morning. Richard is taking me to lunch.

PAUL: Right. Have a nice time.

RICHARD: We intend to. Thank you.

(*Charlotte and Richard exit to the street. A moment later, Ethel hurries in from above carrying a pair of trousers and hurries down the stairs*)

PAUL: Ethel, have you seen George? (*She doesn't hear him*) *Ethel!*

ETHEL: *What?!*

PAUL: *Where's George?*

ETHEL: He's right behind me!

(*She hurries across the room—as George enters from above in hot pursuit*)

GEORGE: Stop! Give me those Cyrano pants!

ETHEL: No! I have to let them out!

PAUL: George . . .

ETHEL: They are far too snug, you look ridiculous!

GEORGE: They're my pants!

ETHEL: Your backside looks like a watermelon!

GEORGE: Nobody asked you!

(*He grabs the pants and they struggle over them*)

PAUL: George!

ETHEL: They need fixing!

GEORGE: Your ears need fixing!

(*Rrrrrip! They rip down the middle, at the crotch.
George and Ethel are each left with a leg*)

ETHEL: Now look what you've done. (*She takes George's
leg and heads for the door*) No wonder this company
is going down the toilet.

(*She exits. George screams with frustration*)

PAUL: George, I have some bad news.

GEORGE: What? Bad news in this company? The House
of Usher Repertory Theatre?

PAUL: I think you better sit down.

GEORGE: "Sit down?" Because I'll tremble? My knees will wobble uncontrollably? That is a stage convention, you idiot, out of the cheapest melodrama!

PAUL: George, Eileen is pregnant.

(*Beat. George's knees start to wobble, and he sits down*)

GEORGE: Oh my God.

PAUL: She says you slept together in Detroit and now she's pregnant.

GEORGE: That's a lie!

PAUL: You didn't sleep with her?

GEORGE: . . . It was Cincinnati.

PAUL: I think that's irrelevant.

GEORGE: Holy Mother of God. Charlotte will kill me.

PAUL: I know.

GEORGE: She'll make my life a living hell! *More than usual!* (*He holds his head and groans*) What can I do?

PAUL: . . . Run?

GEORGE: Think of something, you idiot! That's what you're paid for!

PAUL: All right, all right. Let me think . . . (*He makes it up as he goes along*) Okay. Now listen. . . . Eileen could have the baby . . . in the country. With a relative, like an aunt or something. And we won't tell Charlotte, ever! And . . . you could take trips every few months and . . . and visit them in the country and have picnics, and . . . *then*, when the baby is like . . . ten years old, you could cast her as the Page in *Much Ado About Nothing*, and you could put on shows together!

GEORGE: . . . I need help, not Mickey Rooney!

PAUL: Sorry. Look maybe you should talk to Eileen.

GEORGE: Eileen. Oh my God. The poor kid. I'd better go see her.

PAUL: You'll have to hurry. She has a doctor's appointment at noon.

GEORGE: Already?

PAUL: They have to do a test or something.

GEORGE: . . . What test?

(*The following section goes rapidly*)

PAUL: I don't know.

GEORGE: A pregnancy test?

PAUL: I have no idea.

GEORGE: So she might not be pregnant?

PAUL: She says she's positive.

GEORGE: But she only *thinks* she's pregnant?

PAUL: She's positive! She thinks.

GEORGE (*shaking Paul*): *Christ Almighty, is she pregnant or isn't she?!*

PAUL: *I don't know, George, I didn't examine her!*

(*Charlotte suddenly enters from the street . . . and the two men instantly assume a pose of studied nonchalance and freeze*)

CHARLOTTE: It's chilly out there. I'm getting a wrap and then I'll be back around one.

GEORGE: Good. Great.

CHARLOTTE: By the way. Richard is here. He's taking me to lunch.

GEORGE: Bon appétit.

(*Charlotte exits to the dressing rooms, slamming the door behind her*)

GEORGE: Oh my God. What if Eileen talks to her?

PAUL: I doubt that.

GEORGE: Go in there and keep them separated. I have to think.

PAUL: She's going to find out sooner or later . . .

GEORGE: *Would you do what I'm telling you!*

(*Paul exits. George is alone*)

GEORGE: Damn damn damn. Piss piss piss. Balls balls balls.

(*Eileen enters down the stairs. She's clearly been crying and is still on the verge of tears, but she tries very hard to smile through it*)

EILEEN: Hi, George.

GEORGE: Eileen!

EILEEN: I guess Paul told you.

GEORGE: He did. Yes. Eileen. What can I say? What can I *do?*

EILEEN: I think you did it already, George.

GEORGE: Eileen, I'm so sorry. We got carried away.

EILEEN: I was such a fool!

GEORGE: We were both fools.

EILEEN (*breaking down*): And now we're having a little fool! Oh, George . . .

GEORGE (*comforting her—but also afraid of discovery*): Eileen . . . shh . . .

EILEEN: I hope he looks just like you!

GEORGE: Oh, my God!

EILEEN: I can't do the matinee today. I'm sorry.

GEORGE: But you don't have an understudy.

EILEEN: Well I can't do it! I'd still be at the doctor's anyway.

GEORGE: The doctor's. For a test . . . (*She nods*) To confirm that you are . . .

EILEEN: That's right.

GEORGE: So then you might not actually be . . .

EILEEN: I'm pregnant, George. Believe me. I'm two weeks late, and I've been tossing my guts up every morning for three days. What do you think it is?!

GEORGE: . . . Bad oyster?

EILEEN: I'll see you later.

(*She starts to leave*)

GEORGE: Eileen. You, uh, didn't tell Charlotte, did you?

EILEEN: I haven't seen her . . .

GEORGE: Good!

(*He walks away . . .*)

EILEEN: So I left her a note.

(*And he trips*)

GEORGE: . . . What?!

EILEEN: Well she has to know some time! I mean, she's gonna figure it out when I start waddling around here like a duck! "Romeo, Romeo, Quack quack quack quack." Anyway, I scribbled it down on something. I think it was her copy of *Variety*.

GEORGE: *Variety?*

EILEEN: I've got to go now, George.

(*She exits*)

GEORGE: Holy Mother of God.

(*Paul enters*)

PAUL: George, I couldn't find Eileen anywhere . . .

GEORGE: Paul! Go to Charlotte's room, quick, and bring me her copy of *Variety!*

PAUL: George, there's a copy of *Variety* right here.

GEORGE: I don't want to read it, you idiot!!

(*Charlotte enters with a copy of* Variety)

CHARLOTTE (*all smiles*): Hello, George. Hello, Paul.

PAUL/GEORGE: Hi.

CHARLOTTE: Paul, would you excuse us for a few minutes?

PAUL: Sure.

GEORGE (*to Paul*): Stay where you are!

CHARLOTTE: Leave the room, Paul.

PAUL: Yes, ma'am.

(*He exits at a run*)

CHARLOTTE (*still smiling*): George, the strangest item appeared in this week's *Variety*.

GEORGE: Charlotte . . .

CHARLOTTE: I think you should read it, George. Out loud. You see, I might just be having a menopausal hallucination.

GEORGE: Charlotte . . .

CHARLOTTE: Read it, dear. Near the top. I'm waiting.

GEORGE (*takes the paper; reads*): . . . "Box Office Biggie Boffo in Burbs."

CHARLOTTE: Below that.

GEORGE: "Dear Charlotte. I'm carrying your husband's . . . piles. Files?"

CHARLOTTE: "Child!" "I'm carrying your husband's *child!*"

GEORGE: Right. "I thought you should know. Eileen."

(*She takes back the paper*)

CHARLOTTE: Well?

(*He drops to his knees*)

GEORGE: Charlotte, I am profoundly sorry! I made a grievous mistake. Can you forgive me?

(*He bows his head*)

CHARLOTTE: No, George! (*She whacks him with the paper*) I can*not* forgive you! (*Whack!*) You betrayed me! (*Whack!*) After thirty-five years!

(*Whack whack whack whack*)

GEORGE: Ow! Ow! Ow! Ow!

(*At this moment, Eileen enters from the street and hurries across the room*)

EILEEN: Sorry. I left something upstairs.

(*Charlotte resumes whacking George with the paper, and Eileen turns back*)

EILEEN: Charlotte, I'm sorry. But you shouldn't blame George. It was all my fault. I guess I shouldn't have believed him when he said that next season *I* could play Roxane.

(*Pause. Charlotte turns and looks at George*)

EILEEN: Sorry.

(*And Eileen exits to the dressing rooms*)

CHARLOTTE: . . . Roxane? . . . *Roxane?!!*

GEORGE: Charlotte, listen. Please. It was right after a performance and I was filled with all that passion for Cyrano. I lost my head.

CHARLOTTE: You lied to me.

GEORGE: I didn't want to! You cornered me!

CHARLOTTE: Don't touch me.

GEORGE: Charlotte, I'm flesh and blood! Did you expect me to be celibate all my life?!

CHARLOTTE: Three days! You couldn't be celibate for *three days?!*

(*She starts hitting him again, and he wrestles her down onto the chaise*)

GEORGE: Stop it . . . stop it . . . would you please . . . (*She's down on her back and he's standing in front of her*) All right?! Now will you stop it?!

(Beat. Then she kicks him hard in the groin. He gasps with pain. Then she stands up, straightens her dress and heads for the door to her dressing room)

CHARLOTTE: I'm leaving with Richard on the next plane.

GEORGE: *Wait!* (*She pauses*) We have a matinee.

CHARLOTTE (*the last straw*): . . . Good-bye, George. I have to pack.

GEORGE: *Charlotte!*

(She exits, slamming the door, and Paul enters from backstage)

PAUL: Well? How'd it go? (*George looks at him*) Not well. (*George sits*) George? (*No response*) George, would you say something?

GEORGE (*with great bitterness*): I'm a hack. I was always a hack and now I'm a bigger hack. I have sunk to new depths of hackdom.

PAUL: George, come on. You can't give up. What about all your fans?

GEORGE: My fans? (*He laughs*) Fine. I'll call one, you call the other.

PAUL: George, you made a mistake. Everybody makes mistakes. Let me talk to her. She'll listen to me.

GEORGE: It's too late, Horatio. Just cancel the performance for this afternoon. In fact, cancel the whole tour.

PAUL: You can't do that. You'll get sued.

GEORGE: Let the bastards sue me! Let them nail me to a cross! God knows I've suffered enough.

(*The phone rings, and Paul grabs it*)

PAUL: Hello?! . . . (*Covering the receiver, to George*) It's your agent from New York.

GEORGE: I'm not here.

PAUL (*into the phone*): He's right here. (*To George*) Would you talk to him!

(*George snatches the phone*)

GEORGE: Hello, Henry. How's the blood-sucking business? . . . All right, I'm listening! . . . Well of course I know they started filming yesterday. I have a little Ronald Colman doll that I'm sticking pins into. . . . What? . . . You're joking.

(*The tone of the conversation changes completely now; something incredibly wonderful has happened and George becomes increasingly euphoric*)

GEORGE: . . . Henry, if this is a joke, I'll kill you. . . . Oh, my God! *I don't believe it!*

PAUL: What happened?

GEORGE (*to Paul*): Shh. (*Into the phone*) . . . Oh, my God, that's wonderful! Henry, I love you!

PAUL: George, what happened?

GEORGE: Would you shut up! (*Into the phone*) . . . Today? . . . Yes, of course I'll be here. . . . Right. I'll call you.

(*He hangs up*)

PAUL: Well?

GEORGE (*beside himself with excitement*): We're back in business. (*Calling through the door*) *Charlotte, get in here!*

PAUL: *What happened?!!*

GEORGE: Yesterday, on the set of *The Twilight of The Scarlet Pimpernel,* Ronald Colman made his first entrance . . . and fell down a flight of stairs and broke his legs.

PAUL: Oh my God . . .

GEORGE: As a consequence, the director of the film, Frank Capra, winner of two thousand Academy Awards, Mr. Hollywood himself, is flying here to watch the matinee.

PAUL: Frank Capra?

GEORGE: *Ha haaaa!*

(*Charlotte enters, carrying a suitcase, and heads straight for the street door*)

CHARLOTTE: Good-bye, George.

GEORGE (*intercepting her*): Yes yes yes. I'm sorry.

CHARLOTTE: George!

GEORGE: Now listen. The most wonderful thing in the world has happened: Ronald Colman is crippled!

CHARLOTTE: What?

GEORGE: Henry just called. It seems that Mister Colman made a most dramatic entrance yesterday on the set of *The Scarlet Pimpernel* by careening head first down a flight of steps. (*With great relish*) I'll bet it was the tights that got him, apparently, in both of his legs. Not one. (*Ecstatic*) *Both!*

CHARLOTTE: Henry told you this.

GEORGE: The studio is desperate! Every minute they delay is costing a fortune. So, what director do you think is on a plane this very second heading for Buffalo, New York? I'll give you a hint. (*Cheerleading*) Give me a C. *C!* Give me an A. *A!* Give me a P. *P!*

CHARLOTTE: George . . .

GEORGE: I know what you're thinking, Charlotte. Where do you fit into all this. Well, if I do get the role, and it's beginning to look extremely likely, I will insist that you play Marguerite.

CHARLOTTE: I don't know what to say, George.

GEORGE (*bows his head*): I know. I'm a saint.

CHARLOTTE: Except this is easily the most ridiculous lie you have ever told me.

GEORGE: . . . What?

CHARLOTTE: Good-bye, George. Take care of yourself.

(*She picks up her suitcase and starts to exit*)

GEORGE/PAUL: *Stop! Wait!*

GEORGE (*incredulous*): You don't believe me?

CHARLOTTE: George . . .

GEORGE: There are fractures.

CHARLOTTE: Oh, George, please . . .

GEORGE: Wait! Charlotte, you must believe me. Have I ever lied to you before?

(*She staggers—then exits*)

CHARLOTTE: Good-bye, George.

(*He runs after her*)

GEORGE (*off*): Charlotte! Charlotte, please!

CHARLOTTE (*off*): *I said good-bye!!!*

(*We hear a crash, off. Charlotte has hit George with the suitcase*)

GEORGE (*off*): *Ooowww!!!*

(*George reenters, limping badly*)

GEORGE: *Ahh! Ahh! Ahh!*

PAUL: George? . . . George . . . ?

GEORGE: I'm going to kill myself. No! That's too easy. I'm going to get very, very drunk, and *then* I'll kill myself.

(*Ethel enters carrying George's Cyrano pants*)

ETHEL: There you are. Well I'm glad to say they're finished. No thanks to you. Now try them on. (*She throws the trousers onto George's lap. George stares at her blankly*) Go ahead! I'll turn around. Puh. As if you're modest. That'll be the day.

(*George looks at the pants—then winds them around his hands as if to strangle her*)

PAUL: George, give me the pants . . .

GEORGE: No.

PAUL: George!

GEORGE: They can give me the chair. It'll be worth it.

PAUL (*grabbing the pants*): Now stop it!

GEORGE: Let me go!

(*They struggle over the pants. Then, rrrrrip! They rip the pants in half again*)

GEORGE: *Goddammit to hell!!!*

(*George throws the pants to the ground and jumps up and down on them. Ethel turns around. The phone rings. And Roz enters from the street*)

ETHEL: I don't believe it.

ROZ: Daddy! What's wrong?!

PAUL: Roz!

ROZ: Paul?!

(*Ring! George stalks out, heading for his dressing room*)

GEORGE (*exiting*): *Ahhhhhh!*

ROZ: Daddy! Where are you going?!

PAUL: George!

ETHEL: He has finally gone completely insane!

(*Ring!*)

PAUL (*into the phone*): Yes?! . . . Hold on. (*He runs to the door and calls off*) George! It's Capra's New York office! What do I tell them?! George!

(*No response*)

ROZ: Paul, what's going on?

PAUL: That's a very good question. (*Into the phone*) Hi.
He's in a meeting. Could Mr. Capra come tomorrow?

ROZ: Frank Capra?

PAUL (*nods to Roz and continues on the phone*): He's on
his way to the airport. Right. (*He hangs up*) . . .
Holy God!

ROZ: Paul, what happened?!

PAUL: Come on, we have to stop him!

(*Paul grabs Roz by the hand and pulls her out the door
to the dressing rooms to find George*)

PAUL: *George!*

(*They're gone—leaving Ethel alone onstage, sitting,
sewing up the Cyrano pants. An instant later, Charlotte
hurries in from the street, followed by Richard. She's
carrying a newspaper*)

RICHARD: Charlotte, what are you doing?!

CHARLOTTE (*calling*): George . . . ! *George!*

RICHARD: You buy a newspaper and you go berserk.

CHARLOTTE: Read that.

RICHARD: "Earthquake in Guatemala. Thousands killed—"

CHARLOTTE (*with scorn*): Not that. *That.*

RICHARD: "Disaster at MGM. Colman on Crutches. Garson Walks Out."

CHARLOTTE (*a maniacal gleam in her eye*): She walked out. (*Then*) Mother? (*No response*) Mother?!

ETHEL: What?

CHARLOTTE: *Where's George?*

ETHEL: I hope he's getting a root canal.

CHARLOTTE (*heading through the door to the dressing rooms*): Richard, come on.

RICHARD: I'd rather not.

CHARLOTTE: Richard!

RICHARD: Oh. Right. Coming.

CHARLOTTE (*off*): George!

(*They're gone—at which moment, Paul and Roz enter through another door*)

PAUL: George . . . ?

ROZ: Grandma. (*No response*) *Grandma!*

ETHEL: What?!

ROZ: *Have you seen Daddy?*

ETHEL: Too many times. Your mother's looking for him too.

ROZ: Mother?

PAUL: Charlotte's back? Oh great! This is great! *Ethel, where did she go?*

ETHEL (*pointing*): Through there. (*The door to the dressing rooms*)

PAUL: Come on.

ROZ (*hurrying off after Paul*): This is why I left the theatre.

PAUL: Would you come on! . . . Charlotte!

(*Paul and Roz exit—at which moment, Charlotte and Richard enter through another door*)

CHARLOTTE: George! . . . He has to be here someplace. . . . *Mother?!*

ETHEL (*pointing*): Through there. (*The door to the dressing rooms*)

CHARLOTTE: Richard, come on!

RICHARD: I find this very tiresome.

CHARLOTTE (*off*): George!

(*They're gone—and Paul enters through another door*)

PAUL: Roz . . . ?

ETHEL (*pointing*): Through there. (*The door to the dressing rooms*)

PAUL: Now I lost Roz.

(*And Eileen enters from the top of the stairs*)

PAUL: Eileen! Have you seen George!

EILEEN (*crying, heading for the street door*): No, and I never want to see him again as long as I live!

(*She's gone*)

PAUL: Oh, hell. (*Exiting through the door to the dressing rooms*) Roz?! George?! Charlotte?!

(*He's gone . . . and Roz enters through another door*)

ROZ: Paul?

ETHEL (*pointing*): Through there. (*The door to the dressing rooms*)

(*Howard enters from the street*)

HOWARD: Roz, I've been looking all over for you!

ROZ: Howard . . .

HOWARD: I'm ready, I can meet your parents.

ROZ: Not now, you can meet them later. (*She closes the door in his face and runs off, calling*) Paul?! Daddy?! Mother?!

(*She's gone—and George enters at the top of the stairs carrying a bottle of Scotch and an envelope*)

GEORGE: Ethel!

ETHEL: What?!

GEORGE: When you see Rosalind, give her this letter.

ETHEL: I am not your personal slave.

GEORGE: Give it to her *or I'll have you killed!*

ETHEL (*taking it*): Oh all right!

GEORGE (*exiting to the street*): Where the hell is the Mafia when you need them.

(*He's gone . . . and Paul and Roz hurry on through different doors*)

PAUL/ROZ: George?!/Daddy?! (*They see each other*) Roz!/Paul!

PAUL: Did you find him?

ROZ: No.

PAUL: He's got to be here somewhere!

ETHEL: Oh, Rosalind, this is for you. It's from Mr. Potatohead.

ROZ (*she takes the letter and tears it open*): "Dear Roz, Don't worry about me, I'll be back in a few days." A *few days?!*

PAUL: Oh my God!

(*Charlotte and Richard enter*)

CHARLOTTE: Roz! I can't find your father . . .

ROZ: Mother . . .

CHARLOTTE: Wait. I'll bet he's at the hotel.

PAUL: Charlotte . . .

CHARLOTTE: Paul, Paul, Paul. Guess what?! He was telling the truth! Capra *is* coming to the matinee!

ROZ/PAUL: Mother/Charlotte . . .

CHARLOTTE: Do you realize what this means?! (*From the depths of her being*) No more Apache Woman. I'm going to be a *big star* . . . *!*

PAUL/ROZ: Charlotte!/Mother!

(*Charlotte begins doing an Indian Dance of Joy*)

CHARLOTTE: Hiya hiya hiya hiya! Woop woop woop woop!

ROZ: *Mother!* Would you *listen!* (*Charlotte stops*) Daddy left me a note. I think you should read it.

CHARLOTTE: Okay! (*Happily*) "Dear Roz, Don't worry about me, I'll be back in a few days. Love, Daddy." Fine!

(*She hands the letter back to Roz . . . and then it sinks in*)

CHARLOTTE (*screams—and falls back into the arms of Paul and Roz*): Noooooooooo!!!!

(*Quick fade to black. End of Act One.*)

ACT TWO

Scene One

The green room, about two hours later. Roz is sitting in front of a telephone and a phone book. Paul is pacing nervously, upset. They both look frazzled.

PAUL: I don't believe this. . . . I don't believe it!

ROZ: Paul . . .

PAUL: How could your father just disappear? I mean, my God, Frank Capra?!

ROZ: Paul!

PAUL: Don't you have any ambition left? I mean, this could be it, for all of us!

ROZ: Don't you ever think about anything but acting?

PAUL: . . . Sure. Directing. I could direct. I've also written a play that happens to have a terrific part for you in it.

ROZ: Excuse me, but I have a life . . .

PAUL *(looks around)*: This isn't a life? Wait, I'm breathing. I think it's a life . . .

ROZ: Paul, not now! I want to find my father!

PAUL: Well, so do I! (*Pause*) Are you sure we called *all* the bars?

ROZ: I'm positive. I checked them off.

PAUL: I still can't picture your father getting drunk. I've never seen him take a drink in all these years.

ROZ: He only drinks when he's under great stress. The night I went out on my first date, he drank an entire bottle of vermouth. Then he followed me around disguised as an Irishman. It was like being stalked by Eugene O'Neill.

(*Charlotte drags in from the street*)

PAUL/ROZ: Well?!

CHARLOTTE: He's still not at the hotel. The manager has alerted the staff, and they'll call us if he shows up.

PAUL: I don't believe this!

CHARLOTTE: *You* don't believe it?!

ROZ: I believe it.

CHARLOTTE: How could he do this to me?!!

ROZ: It's not his fault.

CHARLOTTE: Of course it's his fault, Rosalind! Don't defend him!

ROZ: But *you* walked out on *him.*

CHARLOTTE: Which I wouldn't have done if he hadn't lied to me.

ROZ: Well you must have driven him to it.

CHARLOTTE: . . . *I* drove *him* to it?

ROZ: Well you must have.

CHARLOTTE (*staggered*): This is what I get . . . for four days of the worst labor in the history of medicine? "I must have?!"

ROZ: Oh, Mother, don't get dramatic.

CHARLOTTE: Do you know how big your head was?!

(*The phone rings. Paul grabs it*)

PAUL: Hello! . . . Yes it is. . . . Great! (*To the others, excited*) It's the Paramount Bar, on Delaney. They think George just walked in.

ROZ/CHARLOTTE: Great!/Thank God!

PAUL (*into the phone*): Now listen, can you keep him there? . . . Oh. Hold on. (*To the others*) He wants to know if there's a reward.

CHARLOTTE: Oh for God . . .

ROZ: Tell him two tickets to *Private Lives.*

PAUL (*into the phone*): Two tickets to *Private Lives.*

ROZ: With dinner afterwards.

PAUL (*into the phone*): With dinner afterwards. . . .
(*Beat; to the others*) He wants free parking.

ROZ (*grabbing the phone; a killer*): Listen to me, you
pinhead! You want a reward?! Well you keep him
there for the next ten minutes and I *won't* tear your
heart out!! . . . *Fine!*

(*She slams down the phone*)

CHARLOTTE (*shaking Roz's hand*): Atta girl.

PAUL: I'll go.

CHARLOTTE: No, I know where Delaney is. I'll be right
back.

(*Charlotte exits to the street*)

ROZ: . . . Do you see what I mean?! About the theatre?! I'm back here for three hours and I'm acting
like a lunatic. I'll be in analysis till I'm a hundred.

PAUL: It won't help.

ROZ: Oh shut up.

(*Pause*)

PAUL: So why did you come back?

ROZ: I came back . . . to see my parents. Is that a crime? And I didn't know you were here or I wouldn't have come.

PAUL: Well I'm sorry. Next time I'll put up a sign on the Thruway. "Paul in Buffalo. Turn Back. Save Yourself."

ROZ: Okay. Just forget about it.

PAUL: Fine. That's fine with me.

ROZ: Well fine!

PAUL: . . . Let's run your lines and get it over with.

(*He tosses her a script*)

ROZ: Don't bother. I've done *Private Lives* a hundred times. I know it backwards. And I don't see why I have to play Sibyl.

PAUL: Because Eileen took the day off. We don't know where she is. Why don't you blame me for that too?

ROZ: I'm not blaming you.

PAUL: I suppose *I* got her pregnant.

ROZ: I wouldn't be at all surprised.

PAUL: Fine.

ROZ: Well, fine!

PAUL (*opening the script*): Two adjoining balconies. Posh hotel. South of France.

ROZ: I know the play!

PAUL: The lights come up.

ROZ: For the record, I hate this. I swore I'd never set foot on a stage again. I'm breaking a vow here.

PAUL: The lights come up.

(*Roz glances at her script, then delivers her lines totally deadpan, straight out front, with an English accent*)

ROZ: "Elli Elli dear do come out it's so lovely."

PAUL: "Just a minute." Elyot comes out. Your father plays Elyot.

ROZ: No kidding. He always plays Elyot. He's been playing Elyot since I was five years old.

PAUL: He looks at the view. "Not so bad."

ROZ (*deadpan*): "It's heavenly look at the lights of that yacht reflected in the water oh dear I'm so happy."

PAUL: "Are you?"

ROZ: "Aren't you?"

PAUL: "Of course I am. Tremendously happy."

ROZ: "Just to think here we are you and I married."

PAUL: "Yes, things have come to a pretty pass." (*He laughs as Elyot*)

ROZ: "Don't laugh at me, you mustn't be blasé about honeymoons just because this is your second."

PAUL: "That's silly."

ROZ: "Have I annoyed you by saying that?"

PAUL: "Just a little."

ROZ: "Oh darling I'm so sorry kiss me."

(*Beat. Paul looks at the script—a sort of double-take—to make sure the kiss is really there. It is. He kisses her—a peck, to get it over with*)

PAUL: "There."

ROZ: "Ummm, not so very enthusiastic. Again."

(*Beat. He kisses her again*)

PAUL: "That better?"

ROZ: "Three times, please, I'm superstitious."

(*Pause. He leans into her and they kiss with conviction. Then with passion. They really get involved. In fact, they're both getting hotter by the second. He starts kissing her neck and her ears. She's panting for breath*)

ROZ (*hardly able to talk*): This isn't in the script . . .

PAUL: I know. I'm ad-libbing.

(*They go at it again. The following lines come in gasps, between kisses*)

ROZ: Oh, Paul . . . We have to rehearse . . . It's so important . . . to Mother and Dad . . .

PAUL: You're right . . . I agree . . . Take your clothes off.

(*He starts to undress her*)

ROZ: Wait! Paul, there's something important I have to tell you.

PAUL: Tell me later, when you're naked.

ROZ: Okay.

(*They drop their scripts and hit the floor—when the phone rings*)

ROZ: Oh, hell.

(*It rings again. Paul answers it*)

PAUL: Hello? . . . Yes it is. . . . Oh my God!

ROZ: What?

PAUL: Shhh! . . . Right. I'll be right there. . . . Yes, of course we'll pay for the damage!

(*He hangs up*)

ROZ: What happened?

PAUL: That was the manager of the hotel. Somebody walked into the dining room, climbed onto a buffet table and started reciting *King Lear*.

ROZ: It's him.

PAUL: Let's go. We can get there faster if we go through the house.

(*They exit hurriedly through the door to the backstage area. The stage is empty. Then the street door flies open and George staggers in holding a bottle of whiskey. He's so drunk he can hardly stand up*)

GEORGE (*declaiming*):
"They seek him here,
They seek him there,
Those Frenchies seek him
Everywhere.
Is he in heaven?
Or is he in hell?
Ronald Colman
Tripped and fell!"
(*Then*)
I could have had that part. It was mine for the taking. Now they'll give it to some no-talent has-been like . . . John Gielgud. I could play it better than both of them with my legs tied behind my back. Legs, legs . . . ? Legs! Of course! I almost forgot! I should write Ronald Colman a get-well card! Must do it. (*He finds a pen and a piece of paper and starts writing*) "Dear Ronnie. How are the old pins? Hm?" (*He laughs; then*)

"What? Is Brutus sick? And will he steal out of his
wholesome bed To dare the vile contagion of the
night?" Ah, Shakespeare! "To be or not to be." . . .
Big deal. The kid's depressed. We're all depressed!
Dear Ronnie. Did *you* ever play Hamlet, huh? Or
Henry Five? Or Falstaff?! "If sack and sugar be a
fault, God help the wicked. If to be old and merry be
a sin, then many an old host I know is damned. No,
my good lord; banish Peto, banish Bardolph, banish
Poins—but for sweet Jack Falstaff, kind Jack Falstaff,
true Jack Falstaff, valiant Jack Falstaff, and therefore
more valiant, being as he is old Jack Falstaff, banish
not him thy Harry's company, banish not him thy
Harry's company, banish plump Jack, and banish all
the world." That is writing, Ronnie. That is glory on
the tongue, gold on the canvas. It is not the movies,
it is not television, it is the theatre! The theatre! (*His
histrionics have brought him to the call board where
he sees the performance schedule. He reads it aloud*)
"Schedule of Performances . . . Matinee—*Private
Lives.*" Wrong! (*He crosses it out and writes in*)
"*Cyrano.*" (*He looks at his handiwork*) Puh. She got it
wrong again. Charlotte. Dear, sweet Charlotte. She
has the brain of a chicken. And yet, I'll miss her. The
pitter patter of her size twelves. The dainty whine of
her voice, nagging at me like an open cold sore. O, to
return to that midnight hour when you gave birth to
our only child. I can still see you, flopping around on
the table like a tuna on a hook. I can still hear your
dulcet voice, cutting through the night like an air
raid siren. (*Faintly, as if in the distance*) "Please," she
cried, "please, give me the Demerol!" I can't even
tell you now that I love you. Too late. She's gone.
Gone with the wind. (*Bitter*) I would have been excellent in that film. Ah, well. Good-bye, Charlotte.

cellent in that film. Ah, well. Good-bye, Charlotte. Take care of yourself. And it shall be written on his tombstone: (*Almost crying*) "One mistake. He made one lousy, innocent mistake, and they kicked the shit out of him."

(*He trips and collapses behind the sofa, or anywhere else he's hidden from view. Then Charlotte stalks in from the street and slams the door. She does* not *see George*)

CHARLOTTE (*to herself; she wants to strangle him*): George. . . . *George!* . . . You never had good timing, George, but this is incredible! . . . Well. It's over now. Gone. Gone. Gone with the wind. (*Bitter*) God, I would have been great in that film!

(*Roz and Paul hurry in from the theatre*)

ROZ: No luck at the bar?

CHARLOTTE: It wasn't him. It didn't even look like him!

PAUL: Well he may have been at the hotel a few minutes ago, but he's gone now.

(*The telephone rings. Charlotte grabs it*)

CHARLOTTE: Yes?! Yes, I'm *Charlotte* Hay, his wife. (*To Roz and Paul*) It's the police. (*Into the phone*) . . . What? . . .

(*She listens . . . and she turns white and sits down because her knees are weak. This is very serious*)

CHARLOTTE: Oh my God. . . . Oh no. . . . Yes, we'll be right there. (*She hangs up, stunned*) A body just arrived at the morgue, and it fits your father's description. They want us to go take a look.

PAUL: Oh my God . . .

ROZ: Maybe it's not him. Let's go!

CHARLOTTE: Wait! Before we go, I . . . think we should say a prayer.

PAUL: A prayer?

CHARLOTTE: I'm not religious, you know that, but . . . I think it would be appropriate.

ROZ/PAUL: Okay./All right.

CHARLOTTE: Let's hold hands.

(*The three of them hold hands and bow their heads. Pause. Then*)

CHARLOTTE: . . . Does anybody know a prayer?

ROZ: Not me.

PAUL: Huh-uh.

CHARLOTTE: Wait! . . . "God is great, God is good . . ."

(*Roz and Paul join in*)

CHARLOTTE, ROZ, and PAUL: "And we thank Him for our food . . ."

(*At this point, we hear George join in, and then he rises up groggily from behind the sofa, holding his bottle. It takes a beat for the others to register George's voice*)

CHARLOTTE, ROZ, PAUL, and GEORGE: "By His hand we all are fed . . ."

(*They turn and see him, rising up like a ghost*)

GEORGE: "Thank you for our daily bread."

CHARLOTTE, ROZ, and PAUL: *Yaaaaaaahhh!!!!*

PAUL: George!

ROZ: Daddy!

CHARLOTTE (*joyously, throwing her arms around him*): Oh, George, I knew you'd come home, I knew it! (*Reeling backwards, aghast*) Uch! George! You smell like a distillery!

GEORGE: That's odd. I haven't been to a distillery.

ROZ: Oh, Daddy.

CHARLOTTE (*to Roz and Paul, ignoring George*): All right, listen. We have a half-hour till curtain.

PAUL: We can still make it!

CHARLOTTE: First we'll have to sober him up. Give him coffee. Lots of coffee.

ROZ/PAUL: Right.

ROZ: There's plenty here, you know Grandma.

CHARLOTTE: Then we'll get him into a cold shower.

ROZ/PAUL: Right.

CHARLOTTE: I'll lay out his costume, then we'll shovel him into it.

ROZ/PAUL: Right.

(*A loud snore. They look around and see George curled up on the sofa with his bottle*)

CHARLOTTE: George!

ROZ: Daddy!

CHARLOTTE: George, wake up! Oh, for God's sake . . .

(*She shakes him*)

GEORGE: Huh? What . . .

CHARLOTTE: *Wake up!!*

(*He opens his eyes and sees Charlotte, as if for the first time*)

GEORGE: Oh my God, Charlotte, you're back!

CHARLOTTE: Of course I'm back. I've *been* back.

GEORGE (*on his knees, hugging her legs*): I'm sorry, Charlotte. I made a mistake.

CHARLOTTE: We'll talk about that later.

GEORGE: You'll never forgive me, I can tell.

(*He starts to cry*)

CHARLOTTE: George, I forgive you.

GEORGE: No, you don't.

CHARLOTTE: I forgive you, George!

GEORGE: You're just saying that . . .

CHARLOTTE (*shaking him*): *George, stop it! We have a performance in thirty minutes!*

GEORGE: . . . A performance? Well, we'd better get moving.

(*He stands up . . . and promptly falls backward. Paul and Roz catch him*)

CHARLOTTE: Oh, hell . . .

PAUL: I've got him . . .

ROZ: Come on, Daddy, let's go!

GEORGE (*as if seeing her for the first time*): Rosalind! My baby! What are you doing here?!

ROZ: I'm playing Sibyl to your Elyot in the matinee.

GEORGE: . . . Matinee? What matinee?

CHARLOTTE: I just told you!

GEORGE (*as if seeing Charlotte for the first time*): Oh my God, Charlotte, you're back!

CHARLOTTE: *Would you please get him upstairs!*

(*As they help George up the stairs, Ethel enters down the stairs carrying George's Cyrano pants*)

ETHEL: That is the last time I fix his filthy trousers! . . . What's wrong with him?

CHARLOTTE: *He's drunk.*

ETHEL: So what? He always stunk.

(*George tries to wallop her, but Paul and Roz stop him. Then the three of them exit*)

CHARLOTTE (*handing Ethel the bottle of whiskey*): Here. Get rid of this.

ETHEL: What?

CHARLOTTE: *Pour it out!* And make some more *coffee!*

ETHEL: We have a matinee, you know. You should be in costume.

CHARLOTTE: *Thank you, Mother!*

(*Charlotte exits. Ethel is now alone in the room, holding the bottle of whiskey*)

ETHEL: . . . Now why does she want Irish Coffee?

(*She walks to the coffee pot and pours all the remaining whiskey from the bottle—most of a bottle's worth—into the coffee pot, which fills the pot to the brim. The coffee pot is glass, so we can see that the combination of coffee and whiskey still looks like coffee*)

ETHEL: I suppose they're having guests at the intermission. Now in my day, we served strawberries and champagne. Puh. It's only called civilization. Why bother?

(*She puts down the coffee pot—and sees the performance schedule on the call board and reads from it*)

ETHEL: "Schedule of Performances . . . "Matinee— *Cyrano?*" I thought it was *Private Lives.*

(*At this moment, there's a knock on the door; Ethel, of course, doesn't hear it*)

ETHEL: Good thing I saw this. They'd think I was round the bend.

(*As she potters across the room, Howard comes in from the street, carrying a program. He sees Ethel, who has her back to him, and approaches her*)

HOWARD: Hello? (*She doesn't hear him*) . . . Hello? . . . (*He walks around her*) . . . Hi.

ETHEL: *Ah!* You startled me.

HOWARD: Oh, sorry. I'm a friend of Roz. You must be Roz's grandmother. She talks a lot about you.

ETHEL: Young man, I cannot hear a word you're saying.

HOWARD: *I'm a friend of Roz!*

ETHEL: Well, how nice to meet you.

HOWARD: *She left me a note at the hotel! It's very exciting, isn't it?!*

ETHEL: What's exciting?

HOWARD: About Frank Capra.

ETHEL: What?

HOWARD: *Frank Capra!*

ETHEL: Oh. How nice.

(*Charlotte and Paul rush in from the door at the top of the stairs. Paul is carrying George's shirt. From where they are, they can't see Howard*)

CHARLOTTE: How could you lose him?!

PAUL: I'm sorry! I left him in the hall to turn on the shower!

CHARLOTTE: *Mother, have you seen George?!*

ETHEL: You took him up the stairs.

CHARLOTTE: *Since then!* . . . Oh, God.

PAUL: Look, I'll try backstage again. You check downstairs.

CHARLOTTE: Right.

(*Paul exits and Charlotte hurries down the stairs—and sees Howard for the first time*)

HOWARD: . . . Hi. I'm back.

CHARLOTTE (*hustling him to the door*): Look, I'm sorry, but we're busy now. We have a show in twenty minutes.

HOWARD: I know. I bought a program.

CHARLOTTE: . . . Oh, all right! (*She snatches the program from him, takes a pen from his pocket and signs the program*) "Best wishes, Charlotte Hay." How's that?

HOWARD: I-I-I don't think you understand . . .

CHARLOTTE: No, I don't think *you* understand. We're very busy now, so good-bye!

(*And she pushes Howard out the door and slams it*)

CHARLOTTE: These people! They walk right in as if they own the place.

ETHEL: You didn't have to be rude to him.

CHARLOTTE: Mother, stay out of this.

(*Charlotte is heading off*)

ETHEL: I used to know a man named Capra. I wonder if he's related . . . ?

(*Charlotte stops cold*)

CHARLOTTE: . . . Capra?

ETHEL: What?

CHARLOTTE: *Capra?!*

ETHEL: What about him?

CHARLOTTE: *Why did you say Capra?!*

ETHEL: I didn't say it. He said it. He introduced himself. Frank Capra. It sounds extremely familiar . . .

CHARLOTTE (*it sinks in and she clutches her breast*): . . . Oh my God! (*shaking Ethel*) Mother, *why didn't you tell me?!! (She rushes out the street door) Wait a second! Please! Wait!*

ETHEL *(as she heads backstage)*: It's like living in an asylum on the guard's day off.

(Ethel exits; then Charlotte reappears, leading a bewildered, reluctant Howard into the room)

CHARLOTTE: I am *so sorry.* I could just beat myself with a stick! Please, come in.

HOWARD: . . . You're sure? I could wait outside. It's a nice day, which is pretty much what I predicted.

CHARLOTTE: Oh no no no no! Oh, God. You must think I'm completely mad.

HOWARD: Mmmno.

CHARLOTTE: My mother should have said something. The older lady who was standing here. I'm afraid she's just a teensy bit hard of hearing.

HOWARD: "Grandma."

CHARLOTTE: Hm?

HOWARD: Maybe I should call her "Grandma." Heh heh. Or "Granny!"

(He chuckles about this)

CHARLOTTE: . . . Why not?! Granny it is! So. Perhaps we should start over. (*Extending her hand, with enormous charm*) I'm Charlotte Hay.

HOWARD: Hi . . .

CHARLOTTE: Now before you say another word, I just want to tell you what a *huge fan* I am of your work.

HOWARD: . . . Gee, thanks.

CHARLOTTE: "It Happened One Night!"

HOWARD: . . . Well, actually it happens every night at six and eleven.

CHARLOTTE: "It's A Wonderful Life." Wow.

HOWARD: Gee, you have such a good attitude.

(*Absentmindedly, he picks up a paperweight from the table and plays with it*)

CHARLOTTE: "You Can't Take It With You."

(*He quickly puts it down*)

HOWARD: I'm not! I-I-I-

CHARLOTTE: And you're such a young man to have accomplished so much. I had no idea.

HOWARD: Thanks. A lot of people think it's easy. Like there's nothing to it.

CHARLOTTE: Oh, come now . . .

HOWARD: They do! They think it's all just a matter of barometric pressure.

(*He laughs at this; Charlotte joins in—trying to figure it out*)

CHARLOTTE: I'm sure the pressure must be intense these days.

HOWARD: It's pretty bad. But there's a cold front moving up from Atlanta, so that should give us some relief.

CHARLOTTE: . . . Really? Well. Can I get you some coffee?

HOWARD: Mmmmmno. No thanks.

CHARLOTTE: A drink drink?

HOWARD: I never drink.

CHARLOTTE: Nor do I. Nor does George, my husband. The minute we start to work, there is no such thing in the world as liquor.

(*At which point, George bursts in through the backstage door with a new bottle of whiskey in his hand, reeling with drunkenness. He wears an undershirt and trousers*)

GEORGE:

"Once more unto the breach, dear friends, once more!
Or close the wall up with our English dead!"

(He collapses in a heap on the floor. Silence. Charlotte just looks at him, at a complete loss. Then she starts clapping furiously)

CHARLOTTE: Bravo! Brav-o!!

HOWARD *(starts clapping too, trying to be a good sport)*: Bravo!

CHARLOTTE *(confidentially)*: He's been working on this concept for months. Henry the Fifth, the-the-the . . . Pickled Prince.*

HOWARD: He's very convincing. *(Calling to George, who is still out cold on the floor)* That's very good!

CHARLOTTE: Shhh! Please. He's concentrating.

HOWARD: Sorry.

CHARLOTTE: Oh my God, just look at the time. We really must get you to your seat. But we will see you after the performance. Do you promise?

HOWARD: Sure.

CHARLOTTE *(escorting him out)*: And let me say again what an absolute thrill it is to have you here. We're extremely honored.

HOWARD: . . . I have to say, you people are much friendlier than I expected.

* Or "Plastered Plautagenet"

(*He exits, and Charlotte waves with an ingratiating smile*)

CHARLOTTE: Bye bye! (*She closes the door; to George*) You drunken lout!

(*Paul enters*)

PAUL: You found him!

CHARLOTTE: No, *he* found *me* while I was talking to Capra!

PAUL: Oh my God. Do you think he realized that George is . . .

CHARLOTTE: No, he thought the theatre was built on Lake Chivas Regal.

PAUL: Maybe he didn't notice.

CHARLOTTE: Notice? Notice?! If you lit a match in here, the whole room would blow up!

(*George starts snoring*)

CHARLOTTE (*shaking him*): Would you please wake up?!

GEORGE: . . . Oh my God, Charlotte, you're back!

(*Charlotte screams with frustration*)

PAUL: Listen, we'll dress him here. You get his costume. I'll give him some coffee.

GEORGE: I hate coffee.

PAUL: George, please!

(*Charlotte exits up the stairs as Paul pours George a mug of coffee*)

GEORGE: I don't need coffee! I'm fine now!

PAUL (*handing George the coffee*): Just drink it! We have to be on stage doing *Private Lives* in fifteen minutes.

GEORGE: *Cyrano.*

PAUL: *Private Lives.*

GEORGE: The matinee is *Cyrano.* Look at the schedule.

PAUL: George . . .

GEORGE: I just read it!

PAUL: You did not! Look!! (*He snatches the schedule from the call board and reads it*) "Saturday matinee . . . Cyrano?" Who wrote this in?

(*George looks at the schedule*)

GEORGE: No idea.

PAUL: They must have changed the schedule.

(*By this time George has tasted the coffee. He looks at it closely, then looks around at the coffee pot*)

GEORGE: I must say, I have completely underestimated coffee. It is an excellent drink.

PAUL: Is this your Cyrano shirt?

GEORGE: It is indeed.

PAUL: Well put it on. Hurry up.

GEORGE: I have to finish my coffee.

PAUL: *George, we have less than fifteen minutes!!*

GEORGE: Oh, all right.

(*Charlotte hurries in with George's* Private Lives *costume. She sees Paul trying to get George into his ruffled* Cyrano *shirt and stops cold*)

CHARLOTTE: Paul, what are you doing? That's his Cyrano shirt!

PAUL: I know that!

(*During the following, George sits in his undershirt and happily pulls off his trousers, one leg at a time. He has boxer shorts on underneath. Thus, when he's done, he's in his underwear, and his trousers are lying on the floor*)

CHARLOTTE: We're doing *Private Lives!*

PAUL: We're doing *Cyrano!* Look! (*He hands her the schedule*) It was changed.

CHARLOTTE: That's George's handwriting.

PAUL: Are you sure?

CHARLOTTE: Of course I'm sure!

PAUL: Why would he change it?

CHARLOTTE: *Who knows why George does anything?!!*

(*There's a knock at the door. Knock knock knock*)

CHARLOTTE: Oh, God. This is a nightmare! (*knock knock knock*) Who is it?!

HOWARD (*off*): Uh, hi. It's me!

CHARLOTTE: It's Frank Capra!

GEORGE (*heading for the door*): Ah, tell him to come in. I'd love to meet him.

CHARLOTTE (*grabbing George*): No! (*Calling off*) *One second!* (*To Paul*) Hide George.

PAUL: Hide him?

CHARLOTTE: *Hide him!*

GEORGE (*jumping up and down with childish frustration*): Why can't I meet him?!!

CHARLOTTE: Because you don't have any clothes on!!

(*Paul opens a door that hasn't been opened before—the closet*)

PAUL: George, in the closet. Quick.

(*Knock knock knock*)

CHARLOTTE (*throwing them George's* Private Lives *costume*): Just a minute! Coming! (*To Paul*) And put this on him! (*Knock knock knock*) Coming!

(*George and Paul disappear into the closet as Charlotte opens the door to the street. Howard is standing there holding a garment bag with a ribbon on it*)

CHARLOTTE (*all smiles*): Hello again.

HOWARD: Hi. I-I-I'm sorry to bother you . . .

CHARLOTTE: Bother us? You could never bother us!

HOWARD: Gee, that-that's . . .

CHARLOTTE: I was just saying to my husband (*She sees the trousers on the floor . . .*), who was here not a minute ago, I was just remarking how much I love your work. I could watch it all day.

HOWARD: No kidding. Hey! Wait wait wait! Stand here. Watch this. (*He takes a breath*) "The barometer is falling rapidly, and we might just see some flurries by this afternoon." (*Charlotte stares at him blankly*) "So-o-o stay warm, wear those woollies and God bless."

(*He smiles broadly. It was a good performance*)

CHARLOTTE: . . . *Really?*

(*At this moment, the closet door flies open and George and Paul come out, struggling. George, in his underwear, is trying to get out of the closet and Paul is pulling him back in*)

GEORGE: *Take your hands off me! I want to meet him!*

PAUL: *George, stop it right now!*

(*They disappear back into the closet, banging the door closed behind them. Beat. Charlotte is about to speak . . .*)

CHARLOTTE: So . . .

(*when George and Paul come barrelling out of the closet again*)

GEORGE: *I want some more coffee!*

PAUL: *George, put your pants on now!!*

(*As Paul pulls George back into the closet, George manages to grab Howard and pulls him along with them. Bang! The door slams shut and all three of them are gone. Charlotte, who didn't see him disappear, looks around for the missing Howard. Then the door opens for an instant and Howard comes hurtling out. Bang! The door slams shut again. Charlotte acts as if nothing unusual has happened*)

CHARLOTTE: So. What can we do for you?

HOWARD (*completely bewildered; holds up the garment bag*): Hm? Oh. Well, I-I-I have a present for Mr. Hay.

CHARLOTTE: . . . You bought him a suit?

HOWARD: Yeah. No! It's one of his old costumes. General George S. Patton. It came with the helmet and the gun and everything. Hey! I could try it on and surprise him!

CHARLOTTE: *No!* (*She looks at her watch*) Oh, dear, just look at the time. (*She ushers him out the door*) Now don't forget, you come right back here after the show.

HOWARD: If I can wait that long.

CHARLOTTE: *Try.* Just . . . *try.*

HOWARD: Okay. Uh, good luck . . . "Mom."

(*He kisses Charlotte on the cheek, chuckles nervously and exits*)

CHARLOTTE: . . . "Mom?" . . .

(*George and Paul come flying out the door, struggling*)

GEORGE: *I want one more cup!*

PAUL: *George!*

GEORGE: *One cup!*

(*They fall on the pouffe*)

PAUL: *George, stop it!*

CHARLOTTE: George, would you please cooperate!

PAUL: *Lift your leg!*

(*Paul is on top of George, trying to pull George's* Private Lives *pants on over his backside. George's legs, with Paul between them, are flailing wildly. At this moment, Richard walks in from the street*)

RICHARD: I thought I better tell you . . .

(*He sees George and Paul—and reels backward in horror. He had no idea. George and Paul—gay???*)

RICHARD: Good God! You found him! Where was he?!

CHARLOTTE: He just came out of the closet.

RICHARD: Well, I can see that. I had no idea.

CHARLOTTE: Not that closet. *That* closet!

RICHARD: Oh. Anyway, I thought I should tell you, there's a rumor that Capra's in the audience . . .

GEORGE (*seeing Richard for the first time*): Richard?

RICHARD: How are you, old boy?

GEORGE: Paul. Come here. I would like you to meet one of my oldest and dearest friends, Richard Maynard, lawyer, trusted advisor and low-down sneaking *wife-stealer!*

(*George springs at Richard and starts to strangle him*)

CHARLOTTE & PAUL: *George! Stop it!*

RICHARD: *Aargh!*

GEORGE: *You leave my wife alone, do you hear me?!!!*

CHARLOTTE: *George!*

RICHARD: *She doesn't love you anymore!*

GEORGE: *Liar! Take it back!*

CHARLOTTE & PAUL: *George!*

(*Charlotte and Paul pull George off Richard*)

RICHARD: The man's insane!

CHARLOTTE: Richard, I think you should go.

RICHARD: Gladly. . . . And Charlotte: you really do deserve better than this.

(*George springs at him with a cry of anger; but Richard exits and closes the door before George can reach him*)

CHARLOTTE (*to Paul*): I don't understand it. He's getting drunker.

PAUL: Me neither.

CHARLOTTE (*pointing at the coffee pot*): More coffee!

GEORGE: Oh, good.

(Ethel enters from backstage wearing the costume of a 16th century duenna. Simultaneously, Roz hurries in from above. She's wearing a smart evening dress of the 1920s. The two costumes could not possibly be in greater contrast)

ETHEL: Well, *I'm* all ready.

ROZ *(simultaneously)*: I can take over now.

(Charlotte, in the middle, sees them, staggers backward and screams)

ETHEL: Rosalind, you're in the wrong costume.

ROZ: No, you are.

ETHEL: What?

ROZ: *You* are! We're doing *Private Lives*.

ETHEL: No, dear, *Cyrano*. Look at the schedule.

CHARLOTTE: Mother . . .

ROZ *(reading the schedule)*: Look. She's right. It's *Cyrano*.

CHARLOTTE: It is not *Cyrano!* *(Right in Ethel's face)* We are doing *Private Lives, Private Lives, PRIVATE LIVES!!!!!!!!*

(Silence. Slowly, Ethel turns with wounded dignity . . . walks, head high, to the door to the backstage area . . . and with a final, dignified, reproachful look at Char-

lotte, she exits, closing the door. Beat. Then Charlotte, Roz and Paul look around and realize that George is gone. During the argument about which play they were doing, he walked out [carrying his coffee pot and mug] without anyone noticing)

PAUL: Oh my God. Where's George?!

ROZ: He was right here!

CHARLOTTE (*sinking onto the sofa*): Oh, no . . .

PAUL: Now wait. We still have seven minutes.

CHARLOTTE (*lying stricken on the chaise*): Forget it. Forget it, forget it. It's over.

PAUL (*controlling himself*): It's not over. He can't be far. This is no time to panic we can still do the show *so don't panic!!!* . . . Sorry.

ROZ: Now listen. Mother, go put your costume on. Paul, you take the first floor, I'll take the second. And Mother, check the stage before you change. We'll meet back here in five minutes.

ALL THREE: Right.

(As they run out, Charlotte gets hit in the forehead by the door. She staggers with dizziness . . . then exits, straight-backed, trying to keep her balance and her dignity. The stage is empty for a moment. Then the door at the top of the stairs opens, and George walks in, carrying his coffee pot in one hand and his mug in the other. He's half-wearing his Private Lives costume—that is,

*he's wearing the black trousers that Paul pulled onto
him earlier and a starched but askew white tux shirt)*

GEORGE (*thoughtfully, sniffing at his mug*): Beans. It's
the quality of the beans.

(*He falls down the stairs, almost killing himself. At this
moment, Eileen hurries in from the street*)

EILEEN: Oh, George! Thank God you're here!

GEORGE: Eileen!

EILEEN: George, listen! Something awful has happened!
I went to see the doctor a few minutes ago, to get the
results . . .

GEORGE: And and . . . ?!

EILEEN: Yes, I'm pregnant. I told you that.

GEORGE (*starts to cry*): Oh, no . . .

EILEEN: Just listen! As I was coming out, I bumped into
my brother and . . . I don't know why, but I told
him about the baby, and he got *really* upset. He
threatened to kill you.

(*Pause*)

GEORGE: Your brother?

EILEEN: Yes.

GEORGE: Your brother the hairdresser?

EILEEN: Yes!

(*He starts to laugh uproariously*)

GEORGE: I'm sorry. It strikes me as funny, that's all.

EILEEN: George, listen . . .

GEORGE (*laughing*): What does he plan to do? Put me under a hot dryer? (*Really yucking it up*) Wrap my curlers too tight?!

EILEEN: George, you don't understand . . .

GEORGE: Stick my head in a basin and shampoo me to death?!

(*He howls with laughter*)

EILEEN: George, he was in the Marines during the War! He lifts weights! He could break you in half!

GEORGE: . . . You're joking.

EILEEN: He landed at Guadalcanal. He went home to get his gun!

GEORGE: What should I do?!

EILEEN: I don't know. Just . . . be careful. If you see him, run.

GEORGE: How will I know it's him?

EILEEN: He'll be the one in uniform pointing the *gun* at you! Take care of yourself.

(*She exits quickly. George is stunned*)

GEORGE: One lousy mistake and I'm a dead man. Wait! (*He rushes to the telephone*) Hello? Get me the airport. Now!

(*Holding the phone, he peers cautiously out the door. Paul enters and sees him*)

PAUL: George!

GEORGE *(throwing the phone—which Paul catches)*: *Yaaaahhh!!!!!!*

PAUL: George, we have less than five minutes!

GEORGE: Paul, he's after me.

PAUL: Who's after you?

GEORGE: Eileen's brother! He's out for revenge!

PAUL: What are you talking about?!

GEORGE: He knows about Eileen!

PAUL: What?

GEORGE: You know . . . (*He gestures intercourse*) He's sworn to kill me.

PAUL: Oh, George, you're hallucinating. (*Knocking at the street door. Knock knock knock!*) Coming!

GEORGE: *No! Don't answer it!*

(*Paul opens the door—and Howard bounds in wearing Patton's uniform and helmet, brandishing Patton's service revolver*)

HOWARD (*triumphantly*): *Hahaaa! Gotcha!*

GEORGE (*running for cover*): *Aaaaaahhhhhhh!!!!!!*

HOWARD: George Hay . . . ?

GEORGE: Yes. *No!* I look a little like him . . .

HOWARD: Oh, come on. You are so. Well? What do you think? Do I look *tough?!*

GEORGE (*a squeak*): Yes.

HOWARD: Hey! Look at this baby! (*The gun*) Blam blam blam blam!!

GEORGE (*falling to his knees and weeping*): No, please! I beg of you! Please! Don't do it!

HOWARD: Gee, I-I just wanted to let you have it.

GEORGE: I know that! And I am so sorry!

HOWARD: "Sorry?"

GEORGE: I realize that she is young and innocent, and of course you love her greatly . . .

HOWARD: Who? . . . Roz?

(*Beat. Paul and George look up*)

GEORGE: "Roz?"

PAUL: Roz?!

GEORGE (*suddenly angry, the father protecting his young*): What has my daughter got to do with this?!

PAUL: Yeah!

HOWARD: Well, I-I-I-I think she's a very . . . desirable young woman.

PAUL: Who the hell do you think you are?!

HOWARD (*looks at his uniform*): . . . General Patton?

GEORGE (*spitting out the words, advancing on Howard*): You listen to me, you piece of slime! If you ever touch one hair on my daughter's head, I will hunt you down like a dog and pull your heart out through your mouth!!!

HOWARD (*waving the gun in terror*): Stop! Stay back! I know how to use this! I saw the movie!

(*Howard closes his eyes, turns his head and shoots—bang!—and a lamp on the wall next to George explodes. For a beat, George just looks at what's left of the lamp*

*. . . then he screams and starts chasing Howard
around the room)*

GEORGE: You idiot!

HOWARD: I'm sorry!

GEORGE: Paul, get him!

PAUL: I'm trying!

GEORGE: Drop the gun, you maniac!

HOWARD: I didn't mean it!

PAUL *(grabbing Howard around the waist)*: Gotcha!

HOWARD: *Ahh!*

PAUL: Now what do I do with him?!!

GEORGE *(patting his pockets, looking for something)*: Wait a second! Stuff this hanky . . . *(Out of
a pocket, he pulls a handkerchief, which was wrapped
around a Cyrano nose. The nose falls to the floor and
George picks it up. He holds the nose about crotch-
high [Howard's crotch] to see what it is. Unfortu-
nately, under the circumstances, it resembles a sexual
device)* So that's where it was.

HOWARD: *Ahh! Ahh! Ahh! Ahh!*

*(And he faints, leaving Paul with a limp, unconscious
body in his arms. Howard's head lolls from side to side*

like an old eggplant. Paul starts dragging Howard across the room like a sack of potatoes)

GEORGE: Get him into the closet! Here! Stuff this in his mouth! (*The handkerchief*) And tie him up!

PAUL: Why don't *you* do it?

GEORGE: *Because I'm the star!!*

(*Paul drags Howard into the closet—as Charlotte appears at the top of the stairs in a robe with a towel on her head*)

CHARLOTTE: George!

(*George turns, startled, and slams the closet door*)

CHARLOTTE: What are you doing?!

GEORGE: Nothing.

CHARLOTTE: Where's Paul?!

GEORGE: I haven't seen him.

(*And Paul races out of the closet and slams the door*)

CHARLOTTE: Paul! You're not even in costume!

PAUL (*with instant nonchalance*): I know.

(*And Roz runs in, still in her* Private Lives *costume*)

ROZ: Daddy! Oh thank God! Can he do the show?!

GEORGE: Of course I can do it! Just give me a moment.

CHARLOTTE: George, you don't have a moment, you have the second line in the play!

GEORGE: I do?

CHARLOTTE: Hurry up! The curtain is going up in three minutes!

(*Charlotte exits, and Roz turns to George*)

ROZ: Daddy, we have the opening scene together. (*In character*) "Elli, Elli dear, do come out, it's so lovely." Then you come out, onto the balcony, and you say—

GEORGE: "Not so bad."

ROZ (*touchdown!*): That's it! Now come on!

GEORGE: Right!

(*Roz and Paul run out, with George right behind them. As he passes his mug of coffee, however, he stops short and quickly takes a sip*)

GEORGE: It must be Columbian . . .

(*Blackout*)

Scene Two

The stage of the theatre, as seen by the audience. A few seconds later.

As the lights come up, the Act One set for Private Lives *is still getting into position.*

As described by Coward, "The scene is the terrace of a hotel in France. There are two French windows at the back opening onto two separate suites. The terrace space is divided by a line of small trees in tubs." For our purposes, the set should be extremely simple—and rather worn and tacky.*

For a moment, the stage is empty. "There is an orchestra playing not very far off." Then Roz, playing "Sibyl Chase," steps out onto the terrace. She looks very chic, a la 1920s. "She comes downstage, stretches her arms wide with a little sigh of satisfaction, and regards the view with an ecstatic expression."

ROZ: Elli, Elli dear, do come out. It's so lovely.

(She giggles happily. Pause. No one comes out. She looks worried, then catches herself. She smiles and gives a silvery laugh for the benefit of the audience)

ROZ: . . . Oh do come out, Elli. It really is so . . . lovely out here. Just . . . wonderfully, beautifully . . . lovely.

(Silence. Nothing happens)

ROZ: . . . Ell-i! Elli, can you hear me, darling? I do wish you'd join me so we could look at all this . . . loveliness together.

* See Appendix C

(*Roz laughs gaily. Still nothing happens*)

ROZ: . . . *Elli, would you please get the hell out here!!*

(*Silence*)

ROZ: . . . Well. That man . . . I suppose he's still getting into his smoking jacket. Perhaps he had to put it
out first. (*She laughs that silvery laugh; pause*) . . .
Smoking . . . jacket. (*Pause*) Well. I suppose I can
just . . . stand here and look at the lights of that
yacht reflected in the water. My God, I'd like to be
on that boat. . . . And if you were here, Elli, you
would probably just . . . burst through that door,
full of . . . *joie de vivre*, and-and *je ne sais quoi*,
and . . . *que sera sera*, and say something terribly
witty, like . . . "Not so bad!" (*She laughs gaily at
his witty remark*) And I would say . . . you mustn't
be blasé about honeymoons, darling, just because
this is your second. And you'd get very annoyed, and
then I'd apologize and ask you to kiss me. Three
times, because I'm superstitious. (*She laughs gaily,
then glances into the wings and calls*) Elli?! If you're
not coming out, darling, perhaps we should all just
go home!

(*She starts to exit*)

GEORGE (*off*): *I'm coming!*

(*And she reenters*)

ROZ: Oh, thank God I mean my God I'm a happy girl.
. . . Now let's see, where was I . . . ?

(*During the following, George strolls drunkenly, with
confidence, out onto the balcony dressed as Cyrano,
complete with large nose, long flowing hair, rouge,
moustache, leather knee boots, sword, etc. His costume
and makeup are badly askew, and he's clearly drunker
than ever*)

ROZ: I asked you to come out and see how lovely it is,
to which you would no doubt reply, "Not so bad,"
and then I would turn, and gaze out, over the balcony, feeling tremendously happy, and say . . .
(*She sees him and screams*) Aaaahhhh!

GEORGE (*looking around to see what scared her*): What's
the matter? What happened?

ROZ: Elli . . . Elli, darling! How wonderful! You-you-
you-you-you remembered, about the *costume party!*

GEORGE: I did?

ROZ: But what are you doing in your costume *now*, darling?

GEORGE (*taking this as his cue*):
"What would you have me do?! Hanh?!
Seek for the patronage of some great man,
And like a creeping vine on a tall tree
Crawl upward where I cannot stand alone?!
No thank you!"

ROZ (*laughing gaily*): No. Thank *you*, Elli—

GEORGE: "But to sing, to laugh, to dream . . ."

ROZ: *All right, Elli, that's enough!!!* . . . I mean, it's
wonderful that you remembered about the party,
and—and now that you're *in* your costume, there's
simply no reason we cannot just . . . stand here as
if you *weren't* in your costume and chatter on about
anything we please. For example: just look at the
lights of that yacht reflected in the water. Oh dear,
I'm so happy. Aren't you? I mean, just to think, here
we are, you and I, married.

(*No response. George has fallen asleep standing up. His
head lolls on his chest and he starts to snore loudly. Roz
is stunned*)

ROZ: Elli? . . . Elli? . . . *ELLI!!!*

(*She stamps on his foot*)

GEORGE: *Owwww!!!*

ROZ: You mustn't be blasé about honeymoons, Elli, just
because this is your second.

GEORGE: Ow! Ow! Ow! Ow!

ROZ: Have I annoyed you by saying that?

GEORGE: Saying *what?!*

ROZ (*giving him every signal she can think of*): About
our honeymoon, darling! Here in the south of
France. At this beautiful hotel, with the two balconies, where we can lead such *private lives.*

GEORGE: . . . *Private Lives?*

ROZ: That's right, dear. *Private Lives!*

GEORGE (*looks around at the set and finally gets it*): . . . Holy shit!

ROZ (*gaily, mortified*): Elli! Darling! Such language!

GEORGE: I'm in the wrong costume!

(*And he starts to pull it off*)

ROZ: *No!* Elli, it's *fine!* You were at a *costume party!*

GEORGE: Wait! Stay here! I'll be right back!

(*He exits into the wings*)

ROZ: Elli, no! Don't leave me! . . . *Elli!!*

(*And she runs off after him, leaving the stage empty. Pause. Then we hear Charlotte in the wings*)

CHARLOTTE (*off*): *Paul! Quick! Get the hell out there!*

(*Paul comes barrelling out of the wings, obviously pushed by Charlotte. He's playing "Victor Prynne," Amanda's handsome new husband. He's wearing a tuxedo and a false moustache. He sees the audience and quickly stands up very straight and smiles broadly*)

PAUL (*calling*): . . . "Mandy!"

CHARLOTTE (*off*): "What?"

PAUL: "Come outside, darling, the view is wonderful."

(*Charlotte enters as "Amanda Prynne." As Coward describes her, "She is quite exquisite with a gay face and a perfect figure"*)

CHARLOTTE: "Oh, Victor, Victor darling, I'm still damp from the bath. I shall catch pneumonia, that's what I shall catch."

PAUL: "God!"

CHARLOTTE: "I beg your pardon?"

PAUL: "You look wonderful."

CHARLOTTE: "Thank you, Victor darling."

PAUL: "Like a beautiful advertisement for something."

CHARLOTTE: "Nothing peculiar, I hope."

PAUL: "I can hardly believe it's true. You and I, here alone together, married!"

(*They're starting to kiss, when George reels onto the stage, bellowing, with Roz running after him*)

GEORGE: *Where the hell is my dressing room! I can't find the frigging dressing room!*

ROZ: Daddy! (*Then she sees the audience*) . . . Elyot! (*George staggers off and Roz runs after him*) Elyot, come back here!!

(*And they're gone. Charlotte and Paul watch George and Roz go off, then turn around very slowly, back to the audience*)

CHARLOTTE: . . . I knew we should have gone to a better hotel.

(*Paul, as Victor, laughs immoderately; then*)

CHARLOTTE: It's your turn.

PAUL: ". . . Tell me, darling, is it true that you love me more than you loved Elyot?"

CHARLOTTE: "I don't remember. It's such a long time ago, Paul."

(*They both react to the wrong name*)

CHARLOTTE: "Victor! . . . Paul-Victor, to use your full name. Wait! I have an idea, Paul-Victor. I think we should leave here immediately and go straight to Paris!"

(*They start to exit at a run, when George enters coming toward them, trying to pull his fly up*)

GEORGE: *Would you look at this! I can't get the frigging zipper down! What if I had to pee?! Huh?!*

ROZ (*running on after him*): Daddy!

CHARLOTTE: Oh I give up . . .

PAUL: What?

CHARLOTTE: I give up!

PAUL: Amanda, darling!

CHARLOTTE: Oh, be quiet.

PAUL: I beg your pardon?

CHARLOTTE: I said *be quiet!*

GEORGE (*turning at the sound of Charlotte's voice*): . . . Oh my God, Charlotte, you're back!

ROZ (*valiantly trying to stay in character*): "Charlotte?" That isn't "Charlotte," dear. Could that be Amanda, your first wife?

PAUL (*the same*): Then you must be Sibyl, Elyot's second wife.

ROZ: Which means that you're Victor, Amanda's second husband—

CHARLOTTE: *Would you all just shut up!* Can't you see they haven't the slightest idea what's going on?! (*Pointing to the audience*) They think we're insane up here!

ROZ (*not one to give up*): Do you mean up here on the balcony?

PAUL: I love it up here. Just look at the lights of that yacht reflected in the water.

(*At which point, Ethel enters, dressed to the nines as a '20s dowager, complete with tiara*)

ETHEL (*very grand, very British*): Excuse me, but I'm looking for my son, Elyot, who has a tendency to dress up like Cyrano de Bergerac.

CHARLOTTE: Oh, God . . .

ETHEL: You know the English. He used to dress up like Roxane.

CHARLOTTE: Mother!

ETHEL (*deaf*): What?

CHARLOTTE: *Mother, what are you doing?!*

ETHEL (*confidentially*): I thought I should try to straighten things out, if it's not too late.

CHARLOTTE (*hysterical*): Of course it's too late! They all know!

ETHEL (*deaf*): What?!

CHARLOTTE (*pointing to the audience*): I said *everybody knows!!!*

GEORGE (*as Cyrano*): . . . "Nose?" . . . Did you say "Nose?"

ROZ: Daddy! Elyot!

GEORGE:
"Magnificent,
My nose! You pug, you knob, you buttonhead!"

CHARLOTTE (*finally cracking, she screams and runs at George, wanting to choke the life out of him*): Aaaahhh!!!

GEORGE:
"Genial, courteous, intellectual,
Virile, courageous—as I am—"

CHARLOTTE: *Shut up shut up shut up shut up shut up!*

(*As Charlotte tries to strangle him, George grabs her hair and unintentionally pulls off her '20s wig. Underneath, she wears a stocking cap with a little knot on top. After a moment, she realizes what's happened and screams. At which point, Howard, who has escaped from the closet, enters hopping. He's hopping because he's tied up with a rope. However, his lungs work fine, and as he hops across the stage, he screams*)

HOWARD: *Help!! Police!! Call the police!!*

(*Charlotte pulls her wig back on as best she can and beams at the audience, as Howard hops onto the balcony*)

ROZ (*rushing to him*): Howard! Darling! What happened?!

PAUL: "Darling?" What do you mean "darling"?

ROZ: Who did this to you?!

HOWARD: He did it! Him!

ROZ: Paul?!

PAUL: Why the hell did you call him "darling"?!

ROZ: Because he's my fiancé!

CHARLOTTE: Oh my God! She's marrying *Frank Capra!!*

GEORGE (*waving his sword with a grand flourish*):
　"Hark, how the steel rings musical!
　Mark how my point floats, light as the foam,
　Ready to drive you back to the wall—"

(*Acting his heart out, George climbs onto the front of the balcony*)

CHARLOTTE: *George! Stop!*

ROZ: *Daddy!*

PAUL: *George!*

ROZ: *Daddeeeee!*

GEORGE: "Then, as I end the refrain, thrust home!"

(*On his final thrust, there's a blackout, and we hear him fall into the orchestra pit with a crash*

In the transition to Scene Three, as the scenery changes, pandemonium breaks loose. In silhouette, we see Howard hopping around in circles and then off, while everyone else onstage reacts to George's fall)

PAUL: Oh my God!

ROZ: Daddy!

CHARLOTTE: George!

ROZ: Call a doctor! Is there a doctor in the house?!

PAUL: Call an ambulance!

CHARLOTTE (*into the pit*): George, can you hear me?!

ROZ: He's moving! Daddy!

PAUL (*to Roz*): Would you call the ambulance?!

ROZ: All right!

PAUL: I'll go underneath!

(*Roz and Paul exit in different directions. Charlotte is reaching into the pit*)

CHARLOTTE: George, take my hand!

(*We see George's hand reaching desperately out of the pit. Charlotte just manages to get a hold of it*)

CHARLOTTE: Reach! Farther! A little farther!

(*They almost make it . . . but don't—and George hits the bottom of the pit with another crash*)

CHARLOTTE (*calling into the pit*): Stay where you are! Don't move!

(*Charlotte hurries off. Ethel follows her*)

ETHEL (*to George, as she exits*): You're right where you belong. In the pit.

(*And they're gone. By now, the green room has reappeared. Order sets in, along with a depressing sense of peace*)

Scene Three

The green room, about two hours later. The stage is empty for a moment; then we hear voices from outside.

ROZ (*off*): Careful, Daddy.

PAUL (*off*): Watch your step.

ROZ (*off*): Careful!

(*The street door opens and George enters, followed by Roz and Paul. George is still wearing his Cyrano costume, but he's using a cane and looks like he's been through a war. His head is bandaged, and wisps of hair are sticking out from under the gauze. He is not a happy man. In fact, all three of them are pretty low. Pause*)

GEORGE: I have never been so depressed in my whole life.

ROZ: Oh, Daddy . . .

GEORGE: I'd commit suicide, but nobody would notice.

(*George sits heavily on the sofa*)

ROZ: You know what the worst part is? As awful as it was, I actually enjoyed being on stage again.

PAUL: I knew you would.

ROZ: Oh be quiet.

GEORGE: What happened after I fell off the stage? Dare I ask?

PAUL: Well, for a second, after you hit the ground, there was dead silence. Then the audience burst into applause. They thought it was part of the show.

ROZ: Then Mother and I started screaming for a doctor, and some man hurried down the aisle. We asked him what kind of doctor he was and he said he was a veterinarian.

PAUL: That got a big laugh.

ROZ: Then the ambulance arrived.

PAUL: Then the police arrived.

ROZ: Then Howard had to be sedated.

PAUL: Then we all went to the hospital.

ROZ: And that's about it.

(*Pause*)

GEORGE: "Howard?"

ROZ: My fiancé. The one you gagged and locked in the closet.

GEORGE: Ah. And how is your mother taking all this excitement?

(*Paul and Roz glance at each other*)

PAUL: . . . She's leaving with Richard this afternoon.

ROZ: I'm sorry, Daddy.

(*Long pause. They all look miserable. Then George begins to chuckle. Something about this day from hell strikes him as being funny. He starts to laugh out loud. He stops himself. Then bursts out laughing again. He can't help it*)

PAUL: . . . Why does the word "straitjacket" come to mind?

ROZ: Daddy, what's wrong?

GEORGE: Can you imagine the look on Capra's face when I walked out on stage as Cyrano?! He came all the way from New York for that!

(*He howls with laughter; Roz and Paul start laughing, too; it's infectious*)

GEORGE: *He must have thought we were out of our minds!!*

(*All three of them are laughing now. Then Charlotte walks in from backstage, carrying an overnight bag. They see her and stop laughing*)

CHARLOTTE: I'm leaving you, George.

GEORGE (*very sober*): Yes, I know.

(*Beat. Then George, Roz, and Paul burst out laughing. They can't help it. Charlotte, offended, heads for the door to the street*)

GEORGE: Charlotte, wait! I want to talk to you!

CHARLOTTE: There's nothing to talk about.

GEORGE: Of course there is! Please. Just five minutes.

PAUL (*to Roz, taking her arm*): Come on. Let's go.

ROZ: Don't touch me.

PAUL: Sorry.

ROZ (*to Charlotte*): Don't hurt him, Mother. He has stitches.

(*Paul and Roz exit*)

CHARLOTTE: I'll give you one minute, George.

GEORGE: Charlotte, I know how disappointed you are about the movie. And so am I. But is it really that important?

(She looks at her watch)

CHARLOTTE: Forty-five seconds.

GEORGE: Oh, stop it. You can't just leave. And you certainly can't go off with Richard. You would die prematurely. He would bore you to death.

CHARLOTTE: At least he's stable. Mentally.

GEORGE: What good is that if you're bored, for God's sake!

CHARLOTTE: Fifteen seconds.

GEORGE: Would you stop that!

CHARLOTTE: George, I'm sorry, but I have to go . . .

GEORGE: Think, woman! Think for a minute! Use your brain! Think of all the fun we have together. Rambling from town to town like minor royalty. Signing autographs, doing interviews. My God, you'll be laughing about my entrance as Cyrano for months! And think of the joy you give to thousands of people every week. As Amanda and Roxane. Lady Bracknell and Eliza Doolittle. You're an actress, Charlotte. It's in your veins. If you were caught in the spotlight of a runaway train, you'd break into a time step. It's a gift to be that reckless and insane. There are people out there in the darkness who are living through you. Dreaming of what they can be through your voice. Are you really going to turn your back on them because you lost a measly role in a film?

CHARLOTTE: . . . You give me a pain, George.

GEORGE: I know I do. I'm sorry. I can't help it. But I do love you, Charlotte. I haven't the faintest idea why. But the thought of living without you terrifies me.

(*Long pause. Charlotte just looks at him. Then her face crinkles up and she starts to cry. She looks and sounds like a sweet little girl who is crying because she can't have all the candy in the window. This is the real Charlotte breaking through at last*)

CHARLOTTE: I wanted to be a movie star!

(*She sobs on George's shoulder*)

GEORGE (*comforting her*): I know you did.

CHARLOTTE: I wanted to be rich and famous. I wanted everybody to admire me!

GEORGE: I admire you.

CHARLOTTE: Oh, George, we were *so close!* We almost made it. After all these years!

GEORGE: There will be other movies.

CHARLOTTE: No there won't. That was our last chance and you know it. Oh . . . crap!

GEORGE: Perhaps we're not meant to be movie stars. Isn't it nice to know our limitations?

CHARLOTTE: No. I hate it.

GEORGE: I find it rather comforting, now that I think about it.

CHARLOTTE: I don't. I despise it. And I hate getting older. I'm starting to look like Ed Sullivan.

GEORGE: You're as beautiful now as the day we met. No. I take it back. You're more beautiful.

CHARLOTTE: You have glaucoma.

GEORGE (*shakes his head*): Cataracts.

(*They kiss. As they're kissing, Richard enters from the street and sees them*)

RICHARD: Oh. I take it this means we're not running off together.

CHARLOTTE: Oh, Richard. I'm so sorry. You must think I'm hateful.

RICHARD: No, no . . .

CHARLOTTE: Can you *ever* forgive me?

RICHARD: Well . . .

CHARLOTTE: You know I love you, but just in a different way.

RICHARD: I like his way better.

(*At this moment, Roz enters, chased by Paul*)

ROZ: Paul, stop it!

PAUL: You're in love with me and you know it!

ROZ: I am not!

(*By which time, Howard has entered through the street door*)

HOWARD: Roz . . . ?

ROZ: Howard, darling, how are you feeling?

HOWARD: Well, I'm-I'm better, I think, but . . .

GEORGE: Young man, I owe you a profound apology.

HOWARD: That's okay, I just . . .

CHARLOTTE: He thought you were someone else entirely.

ROZ: I still think it's unforgivable.

PAUL: It was a mistake! (*To Howard*) Did I say I was sorry?

HOWARD: *Would you all just be quiet!!!* (*Silence*) I'd like to say something.

CHARLOTTE: Please do.

GEORGE: Absolutely.

(*George and Charlotte sit quietly*)

HOWARD: Roz . . . I can't go through with it.

ROZ: Howard . . .

HOWARD: It's too much pressure! I mean, I'm sure it's just me, but . . . I've never been gagged and locked in a closet before.

ROZ: It was a mistake.

HOWARD: I know, but . . . well . . . something else happened. I met this girl, and . . .

(*At this moment, Eileen enters through the street door*)

EILEEN: Howard, honey. The cab is waiting. We'll miss the train.

HOWARD: Okay, right. I'll be right there.

(*Shocked silence. They all gape at Howard and Eileen*)

GEORGE: Eileen?

EILEEN (*to Howard*): You didn't tell them yet, did you?

HOWARD: I was just, you know, starting . . .

ROZ: Howard?

HOWARD: Well . . . this is a funny story . . . We, uh, we met at the hospital. I mean, we didn't "meet" there, we went steady in high school. Here in Buffalo. Anyway, we started talking and it was like, oh my God, she's so *normal!* (*Eileen takes his hand*) So we went to the cafeteria, for some jello, and then it just "happened." It was like magic. We sort of . . . knew.

EILEEN: Couldn't you just eat him up?

HOWARD: And hey, you know what the best part is? (*To Eileen*) You tell 'em.

EILEEN: Go ahead.

HOWARD: Well . . . she wants to start a family *right away!*

(*Everyone is stunned. Eileen looks sheepish. Howard looks proud*)

GEORGE: . . . What a good idea!

CHARLOTTE: George!

GEORGE: No, wait. Just listen. (*The patriarch, putting his arms around them*) Children. My children. Eileen. Horace.

HOWARD: Howard.

GEORGE: Howard. Speaking for myself and Mrs. Hay, perhaps you would do us the honor of making us the godparents of your firstborn.

CHARLOTTE: And remember: the first one is always early.

(*And Charlotte carefully avoids everyone's eyes*)

HOWARD: Gee . . .

EILEEN: I'd like that George, I really would.

GEORGE: So would I.

(*From the street, we hear a taxi honking its horn impatiently*)

HOWARD: Oh my gosh, we've got to run. 'Bye. 'Bye . . .

(*Good-byes all around*)

HOWARD (*shaking Roz's hand*): I'm sorry.

ROZ (*glum, but trying*): That's all right. Have a safe trip.

HOWARD: Oh we'll be fine. There's a low pressure area over the whole Northeast . . . so we should be seeing sunny skies right through the weekend!

(*Howard and Eileen exit, wonderfully in love. Pause. Roz has never felt quite this discouraged before*)

ROZ: . . . I guess I shouldn't have come back.

PAUL (*bitter*): And you wouldn't have if you'd known I was here. You said it four times.

(*Paul starts to put on his sport coat and leave, as George looks up*)

GEORGE: Roz . . . ?

ROZ: Daddy, stay out of this.

GEORGE: Rosalind. I told you last week on the phone that Paul was here.

ROZ: Did you? I guess I forgot.

PAUL: You "forgot"?

ROZ: Yeah, I forgot! I have a lousy memory! Okay?!

PAUL (*he gets it*): . . . Hey. Come here.

ROZ: No. (*He walks to her, but she backs away*) Paul!

PAUL: I think our first play together should be *Much Ado About Nothing*.

ROZ (*overlapping*): Paul, stay away from me . . .

PAUL: And then *She Stoops to Conquer*, and *Arms and the Man*.

(*He picks her up . . .*)

ROZ (*overlapping*): Paul! *Put me down! Paul, stop it!*

(. . . *and kisses her. She throws her arms around him*)

ROZ: Oh, Paul . . .

CHARLOTTE (*touched, she takes George's hand*): Oh, George . . .

RICHARD: I find this totally revolting.

GEORGE: Family. My dearest family. I would like to make an announcement.

(*Ethel enters from backstage*)

ETHEL: That wasn't a matinee, it was a national disaster.

CHARLOTTE: Mother . . .

ETHEL: What?

CHARLOTTE: *George is making one of his speeches.*

ETHEL: How exciting. Call the U.N.

GEORGE: . . . There comes a moment in every man's life when it is time to step aside and pass the torch on to the younger generation. This, I believe, is such a season for George and Charlotte Hay. (*To Roz and Paul*) To the two of you we hereby present Romeo and his Juliet, Hamlet and Ophelia, Beatrice and her Benedick, those younger roles that your mother and I have now outgrown.

CHARLOTTE: Speak for yourself, dear.

GEORGE: In the words of the man from Stratford:
"This rough magic
I here abjure; and when I have required
Some heavenly music (which even now I do)
I'll break my staff,
Bury it certain fathoms in the earth,
And deeper than did ever plummet sound
I'll drown my book."

(The phone rings, and Ethel, who is next to it, picks it up)

ETHEL: Green room, hams to go. . . . What? . . . What? . . . "Frank?" . . . Frank who?! . . . *(She listens hard, then shakes her head with disgust)* I can't hear a word he's saying.

(And she starts to hang up the phone . . .)

EVERYONE ELSE: *No!!!!*

(Charlotte, who is closest to Ethel, snatches the receiver from her)

CHARLOTTE: Hello?! . . . Yes it is. . . . *(All charm)* Well how do you do. . . . Yes, he is. . . . I see. . . . Well, that's lovely. *(Caressing the phone)* . . . Right. . . . Right. . . . Uh-huh. . . . Good-bye.

(She hangs up. She's so excited, she can hardly speak)

CHARLOTTE: . . . Frank Capra. He said his plane was delayed and he did not see the matinee. But he's in Buffalo now, at his hotel, and he plans to attend tonight's performance.

(Shocked silence)

GEORGE: . . . Oh my God.

PAUL *(murmurs)*: Tonight . . . ?

ROZ *(taking his hand)*: Oh, Paul . . .

(*Silence. Then*)

RICHARD: I really hate to ask you this . . . but which play are you doing?

CHARLOTTE: *Private Lives.*

GEORGE: No, *Cyrano!*

ROZ: . . . *Oh, no!*

(*Everyone starts talking at once, the lines overlapping, as the curtain falls*)

GEORGE: *Cyrano!* Of course it's *Cyrano!*

CHARLOTTE: *Private Lives* is better for both of us!

PAUL: It has to be *Cyrano!*

ROZ: *Private Lives!* I have nothing in *Cyrano!*

ETHEL: I wonder who "Frank" is . . .

RICHARD: Definitely *Private Lives.*

(*They continue arguing, as the curtain falls.*)

Appendix A

On Broadway, we had a fairly complex set, so that the "onstage" *Cyrano* scene was played several feet above the actual stage. Ethel entered on the higher level; then she walked through a hole in the upper floor and down a flight of stairs to the green room. Simultaneously, the raked floor of the upper stage rotated upward to form the ceiling of the green room. This is obviously too expensive for most productions, and the transition from stage to green room can more easily be accomplished in a number of ways.

One way is to have the battle onstage occur behind a scrim. Smoke and lighting will disguise the fact that we're actually on the green room set. Then, as Ethel leaves the "stage," simply raise the scrim and alter the lighting to reveal the green room.

Another way is to cover the green room furniture with drop cloths. Have Ethel walk off into the wings after her first line. Then, after the drop cloths have been removed, she can walk back on through one of the doors to the green room reciting her lines from *Cyrano*.

Appendix B

On Broadway, we found that the actors playing George and Charlotte had difficulty making the swordplay look convincing. Therefore, I wrote a different scene, printed below, which worked quite well:

(*Roz exits. Pause. Howard looks around the room. He spies a Cyrano hat on the table. He picks it up and puts it on. He preens. When he takes off the hat, a Cyrano nose drops out to the floor. He picks it up and looks at it with curiosity—then suspicion. He moves it down towards his crotch . . . is that what it is?! At this moment, George Hay bursts through the center door, still wearing his Cyrano costume, nose and makeup, brandishing a sword*)

GEORGE: CHYAA! (*He sees Howard holding the nose*) Put that down! "You pug, you knob, you buttonhead!"

(*He swats his sword at Howard, who dodges it in terror*)

HOWARD: I'm sorry!

(*Charlotte Hay bursts through the door at the top of the stairs. She's still dressed as Roxane, and she also has a sword*)

CHARLOTTE: CHYAA!

(*George and Charlotte face off*)

GEORGE: "Roxane, interfere not."

CHARLOTTE: "Count de Guiche, you are a villain."

(*They duel*)

GEORGE: "Desist, I say!"

CHARLOTTE: "Never!"

(*George overpowers Charlotte, knocking the sword from her hand. He turns away in triumph*)

GEORGE: "Ha ha! The wench is beaten yet again."

CHARLOTTE: "Dream on, MacDuff!"

(*Charlotte pulls out a knife and throws it at George's back*)

CHARLOTTE: Hiya!

HOWARD (*between them, ducking*): Noooo!!!

GEORGE: Ahhh!

(*George gasps and staggers—and we see the knife sticking out of George's back*)

GEORGE: "Oh, Roxane, thou hast robbed me of my youth!"

(*Dying, he staggers out of the room*)

CHARLOTTE: "Death to the King's enemies! And away!"

(*She exits with a flourish. For a moment Howard is alone onstage, wide-eyed and rattled. Then Roz enters at the top of the stairs*)

ROZ: They're not in their dressing rooms.

When George and Charlotte re–enter a page later, make the following additional change:

ROZ: Howard! Are you crazy?! (*Exiting*) Get back here!!

(*She runs out. A moment later, George and Charlotte re–enter, winded from their exercise*)

CHARLOTTE: Oh, George, you're a genius! The fighting Roxane kills the Count de Guiche!

GEORGE: Do you know what I like most about the author of *Cyrano*? He's dead, so he can't argue with me. (*Charlotte laughs*) Now listen, I have another idea for tomorrow. When the carriage arrives, during the battle, and you step out, I want you to pause, curtsey to the soldiers—and I'm going to put a spotlight on your face to suggest that you have descended like an angel from the heavens.

CHARLOTTE: Oh, George, let's try it! Now!

Appendix C

As with the opening "battle" scene, the change of set to *Private Lives* can be accomplished easily. All that is needed are some plastic shrubs in pots to separate the terraces and a simple railing to mark the edge of the terrace. If possible, a drop curtain at the back to hide the green room and indicate the hotel would be helpful. This is essentially what we did on Broadway.

AUTHOR'S NOTE TO DIRECTORS

In a few places, indicated with footnotes, I've put brackets around some of the dialogue. These brackets indicate cuts that we made in the Broadway production. In each case, however, I think that the longer version can work and, indeed, make the play a bit richer and more interesting—and also provide additional laughs. However, these decisions will vary from production to production, depending on the age and type of actor delivering the lines, the makeup of the audience and the tone of the production. So please feel free to cut these sections (or anything else that you feel doesn't work for you), or give them a try with your first few audiences and, if they work (as I think they do), keep them in.